DEVIL'S PLAGUE

On a summer's morning, a young woman's body lay battered and broken at the bottom of Porcupine Falls. Who was responsible? Was it the local boy, who was so enamoured with her? Or the stranger with the hidden past? And what is the role of the Devil's Plague? It is up to Lynn Hanson and her friend, Victoria Sears, to examine the clues left by the killer and explain the mystery of the death at Porcupine Falls.

MICHAEL R. COLLINGS

DEVIL'S
PLAGUE

Complete and Unabridged

LINFORD
Leicester

First published in Great Britain

First Linford Edition
published 2012

British Library CIP Data

Collings, Michael R.
　Devil's plague. - - (Linford mystery library)
　1. Detective and mystery stories.
　2. Large type books.
　I. Title II. Series
　813.6–dc23

ISBN 978–1–4448–1148–3

For Judi,
And for Deb Ralston and the
burned-out 1957 Chevrolet

Queen Anne's Lace is the wild ancestor of the common garden carrot.

It is also known as Devil's Plague, Wild Carrot, Lace Flower, Fool's Parsley, Bees' Nest, Bird's Nest Weed, Carotte, Carrot, Yarkuki, Zanahoria, Wild Carrot, Garden Carrot, Rantipole, and Herbe a dinde.

1

Redbud Creek eddied around a curving alder branch that drooped low enough for the endmost leaves to spread fan-like across the water. Even though it was midsummer and the leaves were still vivid green, the water's ceaseless flow tugged and worried and pulled until one leaf finally released its hold and floated lazily into the current.

Like a miniature boat, it dipped and swirled its way along the rock-strewn riverbed. For nearly a quarter of a mile, it followed its meandering course. At the top of Porcupine Falls, it caught momentarily against a rock. It caught and trembled, once almost submerged, then broke away, only to tumble down and down and down, into the froth below.

Somehow it avoided the black, ragged bones of dead branches and cutting edges of granite that threatened to rip its delicate surface. Somehow, it managed to remain afloat. *Still whirling — but slower now, slower, with the July sun glinting off water trapped in its shallow cup — it spun through the whirlpool currents of the deep pool at the base of the falls and into the shallows beyond.*

For a while, it rested against an algae-draped stone worn smooth and polished by the timeless flow of water. Then it pulled free again, once more slipping back into the current. It moved sluggishly now, weighed down by the moisture inside. It wallowed along the sedges and reeds that bordered the river until it stopped a final time. Half submerged, its cells began to blacken and to die where they lay wedged between the slightly curving, outstretched fingers of a bloodless hand.

★ ★ ★

It sometimes takes me a while to get used to the absolute stillness of early morning here, high in the mountains.

In the city, especially in the LA basin where I've spent most of my twenty-nine years, it never really gets quiet. Trucks thunder down highways. Airplanes criss-cross in landing patterns over airport approaches. Dogs cooped up in postage-stamp back yards howl all hours of the day and night. Ten-year-old kids rapping at full volume to mystic music spinning through thin wires from iPods to half-deafened ears boogie down sidewalks. Older, even less courteous kids equip low-slung cars with speakers so monstrous that you can *feel* the deep thrumming vibrations of the bass long before you hear the music, even with the car windows closed tight. Mothers yell, kids yell, everybody makes noise.

It's not even quiet at night. There's still the traffic, the ever-present sounds of Southern California transience that seems to clog the freeways almost as much at two A.M. as at noon.

In the early morning, there is the angry whine and clatter of garbage trucks making rounds, the muted roar of cars revving up in preparation for hour-long commutes from distant suburbs to the noise-clogged business core downtown, the subtle intrusion of joggers' hundred-dollar-a-pair Nikes making soft *slap-slap-slap* sounds on asphalt or concrete.

But in Fox Creek — a four-hour's flight from L.A. on a raucous turbo-jet, followed by another four hours by car, the last two twining along a narrow, often-rutted, two-lane road — it is quiet in the morning.

That day, I lay in bed, only half awake, consciously relaxing. Part of me clung sleepily to faint, rapidly fading, but sweet memories of a dream that had, for the moment at least, filled an emptiness I had carried inside for the past year. Another part of me reveled in a stillness broken only occasionally by a barely audible *thump* that might have been a pine cone dropping on the far side of the roof, or a distant *crack* that might have been a branch falling somewhere in the surrounding forest.

Without opening my eyes, I stretched my arms over my head, luxuriating in the sense of muscles loosening, of blood warming my body, of a dream that, while increasingly distant and hazy, lingered on, refusing to die away completely.

Then I froze.

A year ago today.

Lulled by the quiet and the dream, I had almost managed to forget.

A year ago today.

I threw back the hand-stitched quilt that a moment before had seemed a welcome cocoon. Naked feet pressing against the cold plank floor, I stumbled to the rustic bathroom, collapsed against the water-stained sink, and vomited.

Afterward, staring at sparkling water as it swirled the sink clean and flushed away the bitter bile that was all I had managed to bring up, I felt angry at myself. My reaction had been silly and stereotypically female and unconscionably weak. At least, those were all the things that Terry would have said, smiling all the while to let me know he was only joking. Imagining his smile hurt, but at the same time it seemed to help. I filled the glass next to the sink and rinsed my mouth to get rid of the aftertaste.

Still trembling inside, I took a long, hot shower that helped even more. As I stood beneath the spray, eyes closed, head tilted back to let the water finger through my hair, I mentally thanked Estelle and Edgar for their foresight in installing a new, larger water heater earlier that spring. Even so, the water was distinctly cooler when I finally roused myself enough to turn the faucets off, step out, and pat myself dry with one of the soft, monogrammed 'E&E' towels hanging on the oak rack.

Wrapped in the worn folds of the quilted satin robe Terry and Shawn had given me on my birthday a year and a half before — six months before they died — I walked to the kitchen. My legs felt weak and my stomach hurt. I needed to eat something, even if I had to force it down.

Perhaps it was the crisp mountain air or the lingering effects of the hot showers, but the hot whole-wheat toast spread with fresh honey and the mug of hot chocolate made the chore of living through the day seem almost bearable.

Almost.

It had been a year ago. *Today*.

Somewhere, long before, in a half-forgotten class in high school, I had read a story by Hemingway called 'Big Two-Heart River.'

In it the hero, returning shell-shocked from the horrors of World War I, managed to cope with the impossible by reducing every act and motion to ritual. If he could act without thinking, without engaging more than the merely physical part of his being, the story implied, he might survive. He could be like the fish he saw in the Big Two-Heart River — forever swimming against the current, never ceasing to struggle with body and fins, never resting for an instant from their mindless toil . . . and managing, somehow, to stay in exactly the same spot beneath the bridge, never advancing perhaps, but, equally crucial, never falling behind.

By the time I finished my own rituals, mechanically washing and drying the dishes and storing them carefully in the pine cupboard, it was well past eight o'clock.

For this day, I had carefully decided the night before to walk the mile and a quarter up the graveled road and introduce myself to Estelle's nearest neighbor, old Mrs. Sears. I had put it off for the first three days of my stay at the cottage, thinking that what I needed most was to be alone for a while, to think, to mourn. But the prospect of spending hours by myself today was just too much.

A few minutes later, functioning like Hemingway's hero, pretty much on automatic pilot, I was ready to head out. I had dressed in comfortably worn but still presentable jeans, a lightweight long-sleeved shirt, and a floppy straw hat that Estelle had assured me was *de rigueur* for midday walks in the high mountains.

'Don't let it fool you. This time of year, it might start out almost nippy, but by noon, with the sun blistering straight down on your head, you'll be more than thankful for a hat,' she had warned.

Personally, I felt more than a bit foolish about the hat, especially since it was only a few minutes past eight thirty and the air was still crisp, with a lingering coolness that brushed against my cheek when I opened the front door. That, plus I never wore hats in LA — nearly never, I thought, unavoidably remembering my solemn black of the day of the funeral.

But even in the three days I had been in Fox Creek, I had learned for myself that the July crispness could be replaced within hours by a flat, heavy heat made somehow worse by the redolence of pines and dust.

Later, I would be thankful for the hat's shade.

I carefully locked the front door, pausing to reassure myself of the soft metallic *click* of the key, then started walking. The exercise would be good for me, I had decided. The scenery was indisputably gorgeous, with never-ending vistas of ridges topped with dark green, almost black pines and firs, and behind them the mountains themselves thrusting skyward, for the most part barren, grey, and shadowed, but with small pockets of snow gleaming here and there on their flanks. The air felt so clean and invigorating I could nearly taste the freshness, and it wasn't really that far over the low ridge to Mrs. Sears' place.

Old Mrs. Sears' place.

Estelle had made me promise to visit the old woman, and I had agreed.

'You'll never *believe* that woman,' Estelle had said in her rushed, breathy voice. 'She's a marvel, and I think she'll do you a world of good.'

Well, I said half-aloud, half to myself as I walked, my feet crunching loudly against grey gravel, *we'll see.*

I was perhaps halfway from the cabin to the crest of the ridge when two thoughts abruptly surfaced. The first stopped me dead still in the middle of the road. Mere loss became an emptiness so real, so terrifying that I almost doubled over with the pain of it.

I didn't care about the scenery or the fresh air or the cabin or the sounds of pine cones falling on the roof, or any of the rest of it. I only wanted to be alone, to close myself into a small, dark, silent room, and weep. And I didn't want to visit *any* old woman, no matter how highly Estelle or anyone else regarded her.

Out of all the billions of human faces that had ever inhabited this planet, I only wanted to see *two.* But those two were forever locked away from me.

I swallowed and forced myself to start walking again, one step at a time, toward

Mrs. Sears' place, focusing on the second thought. It was eminently more practical and, once I fought back the flood of depression and self-pity, more immediate.

It wasn't quite nine o'clock.

What if old Mrs. Sears slept late? What if I disturbed her? From Estelle's few comments about her nearest neighbor in Fox Creek, the old woman had to be nearing eighty. That seemed a bit old to be living alone, especially this far out from the village, but Estelle assured me that Edgar's family had owned the cabin closest to Mrs. Sears' for years now and that the old woman was more than capable of handling anything the world threw at her, and that I would find old Mrs. Sears a . . . *fascinating* neighbour.

I shrugged.

Better ahead than backward. At least it beat swimming interminably against the stream, only to remain forever in the same place. The emptiness receded a little. I continued up the road.

From the top of the ridge, I could not see anything that looked like a cabin, although the thicker stands of pine could easily have blocked the view. It wasn't until I was almost even with a dirt driveway that I discovered that the road I was on — coarse gravel, with more than its share of unfilled potholes — dead-ended at the edge of a small meadow.

Mrs. Sears' place stood in the center of the meadow. The driveway (little used, if the height of weeds growing in it was any indication) curved around behind smooth log walls. A low picket fence bordered a ragged patch of wildflowers in front before disappearing around both sides. The pickets may once have been white, but they had long since weathered to a uniform and rather pleasant silver-grey.

The gate in the middle of the fence hung from two new hinges; at least, I assumed from their brightness that the hinges were new. At any rate, they didn't squeak when I pushed the gate open and, careful to stay on the sandstone flags that dotted their way across the yard, approached Mrs. Sears' porch.

I stopped on the porch. It ran the length of the cabin but seemed not quite deep enough to do more than provide marginal shade from the midday sun. This side of the house would still get the brunt of the late afternoon light. Already the outside air was warming considerably. Sweat beaded on my forehead and caught in the band of the floppy hat.

Silly hat? . . . not any more.

I took a deep breath. Three days had allowed for some acclimatizing, but obviously not enough. I was winded from the uphill walk. My heartbeat pounded in my ears. From somewhere behind the house, I heard a rhythmic but muted *thunk*, pause, *thunk*, pause, *thunk* that echoed the rhythm of my pulse. The sound was vaguely familiar but I couldn't place it.

So, I thought, fanning myself with one hand, *here I am. I don't want to be here, but today this is as good a place as any* . . .

I raised my other hand to knock on the doorjamb, absently glancing over my shoulder at the yard and fence and road.

The solid oak door behind the screen swung open so quickly and so silently that it startled me.

I must have recoiled unconsciously, because suddenly I was hurtling back-ward, off-balance, one heel half off the edge of the porch and the other fighting a losing battle against my center of gravity. I would have fallen, except for the small figure that burst through the doorway and grabbed my arm with an ease and a strength that surprised me, pulled me back onto the porch and, chattering softly in the sweetest voice I had ever heard, steered me into the coolness inside.

2

The first thing I noticed inside was that the room was designedly comfortable, homey without being pretentiously so, with sufficient light but still shady enough to promise coolness in the warmest afternoon. Framed windows opened on three sides, with lacy white draperies hanging from each window. Plants grew everywhere — so thickly on the deep windowsills that they seemed to bring the outdoors inside, dissolving the boundaries between the two. The greenery gave the room a warm, organic feeling that augmented perfectly the hand-laid fireplace of rough stone and the overstuffed sofa and chair upholstered in deep wine velvet, complete with antimacassars of fine crochet that had to have been handworked.

The second thing was that I was being propelled, supported, almost carried, by what would have been the first-prize winner in any Helen Hayes look-alike contest ever held.

Mrs. Sears — presumably — was considerably shorter than my own five foot six, slim but sturdy looking, with a halo of white hair that, while neat enough, threatened rebellion at the first opportunity. Her cheeks were the proverbial apple red, her eyes a twinkling blue that promised merriment as well as wisdom, and her skin deeply threaded with fine age-lines that concealed while asserting her age. She could have been anything from sixty to one hundred . . . and anything from someone's dearest little old Granny to a reigning queen.

By this time, I found myself sitting comfortably in a deep armchair. My heartbeat had slowed and my respiration returned almost to normal.

' . . . all right, my dear?' I heard Mrs. Sears say.

'I'm sorry,' I said, embarrassed at my momentary and (I sincerely believe) unusual lack of attention. 'What did you say?'

'Are you certain you're all right, Mrs.

Hanson. That was a nasty fright, I'm sure, and for someone not used to the altitude, the walk must have been almost exhausting.'

'Yes, it . . . ' I stopped in surprise. She had called me *Mrs. Hanson.*

'Oh, come now, my dear,' she said, interpreting correctly the cause of my abrupt silence. She gave a small laugh. 'Who else would be walking up that beastly stretch of road this early in the morning.' She pointed at my dusty shoes. 'You certainly didn't ride, and it's nearly an hour's walk past the van Ettens' to the next house on the other side, and that belongs to the Ottleys and not one of them has set foot on my property in three decades. Something to do with a disagreement about hunting rights that led to a nasty little wound — not mine, I assure you — but we needn't go into that right now.' She smiled conspiratorially, as if the small matter of hunting rights was something we women could keep well enough to ourselves. 'And beyond their place, it's another twenty minutes into the village on foot. Who in their right mind

19

would set out that early just to say hello?

'And besides,' she added, her eyes twinkling even more, 'Estelle called me three days ago and told me to take good care of you. She even described you: mid-height, intelligent, vivacious, with dark hair, a generous smile, and — now how did Estelle put it — oh yes, 'eyes that opened like wells onto sadness.''

I laughed self-consciously, totally at a loss as to how to respond to this woman.

'I know,' Mrs. Sears said, patting my hand solicitously and continuing as if any response I might make would be irrelevant. 'Estelle and Edgar *can* be a bit much, but they mean well.'

'Um, yes,' I said, aware of how idiotic I must sound. It would have been nice to actually contribute to the conversation, but so far I hadn't done well on that score.

'Now,' Mrs. Sears said, settling herself primly on the end of the sofa nearest me, 'tell me about yourself.'

And I did.

It surprised me to hear my voice in that softly quiet room, but she drew me out so gradually and so gently that I told her much more than just the bare outline of my plans to spend a few weeks at the van Etten cabin, courtesy of an old friend of my late mother's, Estelle (God bless her for being such a good friend, even though we were not of the same generation and she barely knew *me*), and her husband Edgar.

That much she obviously already knew.

But after a few minutes, I noticed that I was talking about Terry and Shawn — my husband and son who were no more — and the accident and today and my need to be alone but not alone in the house Terry and I bought, not alone in the house where Terry and Shawn had lived, with their memories crowding in at me from every corner. I hadn't spoken so freely about the accident to anyone before, but here I was, opening up to a complete stranger who hunched forward on the edge of her old-fashioned sofa and clucked her tongue sympathetically in all the right places and generally made me feel part of the human race again. The emptiness swelled; then, when it reached the point where I felt that I would have to release it or die, it began to fade, only a little, but enough. The pain was bearable.

'I miss them,' I said simply. 'It's like . . .'

Mrs. Sears never did find out what it was like. Instead, a frenzy of screaming shattered the silence outside. I twisted in my chair, just in time to see what seemed like a hundred small, flitting creatures pounding across the road from a thick stand of pines opposite the house and milling around on the other side of the sun-bleached picket fence, their feet raising billows of dust.

I couldn't understand any words — as far as I could tell, the boys (that was what the creatures finally resolved into, and probably no more than a dozen or so, at that) were just screaming, wild, top-of-the-lung, no-holds-barred, someone-is-slitting-my-throat screaming that echoed through the room.

Startled, I began to rise, but Mrs. Sears was already at the door.

'Those scamps,' she said loudly enough for me to hear and to understand that whatever was going on was nowhere as frightening for her as it was for me. 'I didn't expect them this soon.'

Even as she was opening the door, though, I saw a figure, silhouetted against the bright light, run from the back, past the side window, and around the corner of the house, running hell-bent-for-leather toward the fence. Sunlight glinted harshly from the blade of a huge axe that swung back and forth as he ran.

I must have been more disturbed than I realized; first by the exhausting walk, then by the near fall from the porch, then — most distressingly — by the resurgent memories of violence and death, and then by the eruption of screaming.

I screamed, too.

Mrs. Sears spun on her heels just as I raised a shaking hand and, with all the tremulant appropriate to a melodrama heroine on the verge of fainting (no matter how embarrassing it seems now, I really did it), half whispered, 'He's got an axe!'

She whirled back to the door and yelled to the man at the corner of the house, 'Carver! It's all right,' and then she stepped outside. I crossed to the window in time to see her negotiate the flags and stop just inside the picket fence, fists on her hips, her stance as rigid as any old witch from Grimm's Fairy Tales. The silhouetted figure — whom I assumed to be Carver, whoever that was — disappeared around the back of the house. I caught a glimpse of the axe as the figure passed the side window again.

'Now what's this all about? Can't an old woman enjoy a little peace and quiet around here?' she called to the assorted boys milling about in front of her house. Her voice silenced the tumult at once, but with her questions a second round of yelps and squeals erupted. She laughed brightly and said, 'All right, all right. You mind your manners and I'll see what I can find.'

She turned and walked back into the house.

'Please excuse me just a moment,' she said as she passed through the living room toward the back of the house. 'I didn't figure on them showing up until closer to noon.'

'Who . . . ?' I began, but she was already gone.

Curious, I walked to the front door and stepped onto the porch.

The milling herd had resolved itself into a dozen or so boys, probably between eleven and fourteen, all dressed in ragged, dusty jeans and T-shirts gleaming in various shades of white. They all wore baseball caps, heavy boots, and had packs strapped to their backs, bulging canteens, various bundles neatly bound to the pack-frames, a scattering of fold-up shovels — the kind the Forest Service uses to fight impromptu fires, I supposed — a few sheath knives almost longer than their thighs, and what looked like tons of other supplies.

The boys were obviously headed for campout or a hike.

Behind me, Mrs. Sears rumbled impatiently in the kitchen, while the boys rumbled impatiently along the fence. In spite of their disquietingly abrupt announcement of their presence, and in spite of Carver's concern for Mrs. Sears (why else would anyone come racing around the house swinging a huge axe as if it were a rolled-up newspaper), it seemed clear to me that

25

Mrs. Sears and the boys knew exactly what was happening.

I had stumbled onto a ritual.

'Morning,' a voice called from behind the shifting mass of boys. The voice was deep, mature, and startled me.

A figure stepped through the gate, separating himself from the boys.

'Morning,' he repeated. 'Name's Roy Mintern.' He came closer, holding out his hand. Without thinking, I moved out of the protective shade of the porch and took it.

'Lynn. Lynn Hanson.'

'Staying at the van Etten place, right?'

'Yes, but how . . . ?'

He laughed. 'I'm what passes for a real estate mogul up here. I run maybe half a dozen summer cabins for down-valley folks, and own a few myself. I keep pretty close tabs on who's where. You never know who might want to come up again next year.' He paused and grinned. 'Besides, Estelle and Edgar called me and . . . '

'Warned you I was coming, I know.'

We both laughed. It seemed easy and

natural to laugh with Roy Mintern. He was a decade or so older than I, half a foot taller, with a smile like sunshine on a cloudy day. And he was apparently in charge of the boys — as much as anyone could be said to be in charge of a such a turbulence, no matter that they were struggling manfully — or at least boyishly — to remain patient and quiet.

'My kids,' he said as if confirming my thoughts. He gestured with a thumb over his shoulder. 'Troop 1, the only Scout troop for fifty miles around. Poor things, sometimes I have to rescue 'em from their rough life of swimmin' and hikin' and messin' around all summer doin' nothin' and force them out into the Great Out of Doors.'

We laughed again, and the boys, who must have overheard the whole thing and enjoyed seeing Mr. Mintern flirting with a strange woman, screeched with delight.

'We're heading up for the Falls.'

I must have looked blank, because he continued: 'Miz Sears lets us camp out at Porcupine Falls, along the Redbud, couple of miles or so into her land. It's wild enough to be an adventure, but close enough to home to hike in.'

'You hiked in from the village?' I asked.

He shook his head. 'Not even I'm that much of a masochist. You ever try herding a dozen boys along a county road? Might as well try herding cats . . . and *wild* cats at that! No, we drove. There's my 'official' Scout Van back there. We came up in that.' He pointed beyond the thick stand of pines to a late model van — a nine-passenger behemoth whose original colour had long since disappeared under the effects of bleaching summer sun and scouring winter ice. It apparently came complete with an over-sized luggage carrier strapped on top, and could probably squeeze in another couple of boys or so in a pinch. 'We . . . '

The screen swung open with a *thunk* and Mrs. Sears emerged, carrying a huge tray of cookies and an earthenware gallon pitcher of something cold enough to have formed condensed droplets of moisture on the outside. She had a stack of paper cups crimped beneath one arm.

The boys let out a whoop, then settled

down at a gesture from Roy Mintern, and Mrs. Sears passed along their ragged line, for all the world like a general on inspection, offering freshly baked cookies (chocolate chip — I could smell them a dozen feet away) and a drink of ice-cold milk.

There was a long silence, clearly marking the boys' appreciation for the mid-morning treat, then a chorus of 'Thank you's and 'Good-bye's and a nod from Roy Mintern, and the troop was on its way, disappearing into the pines where the gravel road ended and a narrow dirt path began. Within moments it was so quiet and still again that the whole episode began to feel like a distant dream.

'Those kids,' Mrs. Sears said at last as she stacked the used paper cups inside the empty pitcher, set the pitcher on the tray — now cleaned to the last possible crumb — and headed toward the house. 'I don't know what I'd do if they ever passed me by on one of their Wednesday hikes. Having that bunch stop by is like having Trick-or-Treat all summer long.'

Estelle was right. Mrs. Sears *was* a

fascinating neighbor.

Shaking my head, I followed her into the house.

Half an hour later, we were seated in the dark, cool living room again. I had offered to help clean up the kitchen. Mrs. Sears, who by now was insisting that I call her Victoria and had unilaterally decided that I was *Lynn dear*, accepted the offer cheerfully. We scrubbed up the remains of her early morning cookie making and put everything safely away, then adjourned to the front room.

We chatted as easily as if we had known each other all our lives. She seemed to know that I no longer needed to talk about Terry and Shawn, so showed me her needle work and her albums instead. As boring as the prospects might sound, she made both interesting. She had crocheted nearly everything imaginable, including the gauzy curtains on the windows, the antimacassars on the sofa and chair, and the doilies centered precisely beneath every lamp, every vase holding freshly picked wildflowers, and every lovingly dusted knickknack in the room. She even showed me her work-in-progress, a full-sized dinner cloth that had occupied her off and on for over thirty years.

'Too many other things come up that have to be done right now,' she explained as she spread a corner of the fragile crocheting across my knees. 'And this always seems to get set aside. I try to do a little more each year, usually during the winter when the weather is bad. But if the electricity goes out, I get stalled even then. I can't see to do this fine a pattern by either kerosene lamp or battery-pac.'

I could believe that. Even in the bright summer sunlight, even with eyes barely more than a quarter-century old and possibly half a century younger than Victoria's, I could scarcely see the individual stitches. I fingered the delicate swirls of white thread.

'The pattern is called 'Queen Anne's Lace',' she said. 'It's an old, old one my grandmother taught me when I was a girl. But I've loved it ever since. One of these centuries,' she added with a laugh, 'I may even finish this monster.'

She folded it carefully and returned it to an old cardboard box that she stowed safely in a low cabinet.

'But enough of this. How about a walk around the place, Lynn dear?'

'Absolutely.'

It took a moment for me to get used to the light. It was drawing near to eleven now. The heat was bearing down on the glistening rock showing in patches through the thin layer of dirt in Victoria's front yard. The direct light leached away color until the pines seemed hazy grey-green, and the leaves of the plants scattered in front of me hung pallid and lifeless.

But in spite of that, Victoria's yard was not what I had assumed when I first saw it. Except for the flagstones, it had seemed wild and unkempt, a patch of dry soil overgrown with weeds of every size and shape. But as she began pointing out this plant or that, I realized that this was her garden.

She carefully named every plant since to me they were all strange, foreign. She began at a stand of creamy white yarrow just beneath the corner eaves. 'The best thing there is for avoiding a summer cold,' she said as she pinched off one of the small clusters of blossoms and let me smell its spicy pungency. 'A nice cup of yarrow tea in the evening, chock full of vitamin C to keep you healthy. You can stew the leaves and roots, as well, although to my way of thinking there are a lot of things that are much more tasty.'

A little further on was a clump of gorgeous, midnight-purple larkspur. 'Poisonous, you know, but very pretty. At one time, it was used in herbal remedies, in extremely small doses, of course, but now there are a number of much more accessible — and much safer — medicines to treat those ailments. Rather like Monk's Hood . . . a mixed blessing. I like watching it from my window as I work.'

There were other plants as well. It must have taken the better part of an hour for her to point out the miners' lettuce with its dainty plate-like leaves that she said could capture enough early morning dew to slake a respectable thirst, the minty wintergreen, curly dock, Mariposa lilies (whose roots had saved the early Mormon

33

pioneers from starvation in times of crop failure), wild carrots, currants, gooseberries (the latter two fairly substantial bushes that grew just behind the porch on the side of the house). She showed me each one and told me all about it — where she got it, why she planted it right there, what it was good for.

And the odd thing was that I thoroughly enjoyed the entire experience.

'Well,' she said finally when we finished the circuit of the yard and stood at the foot of the porch steps, 'that's it. How about some lunch?'

'Oh really, Victoria, I couldn't.'

'For goodness sakes, why not?'

'I've taken up so much of your time now that I feel guilty, and I wouldn't want to impose . . . '

'Lynn dear, I have to fix lunch anyway for Carver. And considering how much that youngster eats, fixing for you will be as little trouble as sewing on the last button when the wedding dress is done. No, it's settled. You're marching yourself right inside and sitting down with us for lunch. Unless,' she added, with a

34

mischievous grin and a twinkle that showed through the bright sunlight, 'unless you want to take a page out of Lance Prescott's book and just browse in the front yard.'

I must have looked nonplussed because she smiled widely as if she had made a secret joke.

Laughing, she led the way onto the porch and, while we puttered around in the kitchen putting together sandwiches and salad and iced lemonade, she explained about Prescott.

'You'll meet him soon enough, probably,' she said as she shook the final drops of water from a crisp head of lettuce and handed it to me for preparing. 'He's staying at the old line hut up in the hills. Showed up on my front porch one day — what is it now, two, three months ago. He had a shiny, brand-new Jeep Cherokee chock full of supplies, and asked if he could rent the old shack for the summer.

'He's a city-boy that thinks he wants to be a mountain man. He lives up there with no electricity, no facilities, no heat except a stone fireplace. And every so often he comes down to visit. When he does, he usually ends up eating half my front yard for lunch, putting miner's lettuce in his salad, breaking mustard pods into the soup. Sometimes he is so persistent about making my cooking more 'natural' that I fairly have to swat him out of the kitchen with a broom.'

She chuckled at the memory.

'Why . . . ,' I started to ask, but a sharp rapping at the back door cut me off.

'Come on in, Carver,' Victoria said without taking her eyes off the loaf of freshly baked bread she was slicing into thick hunks.

The door opened and a young man entered. He looked to be twenty or so, but something about his eyes, the angle of his jaw, the cut of his hair where it fell across his forehead, suggested that he might be several years younger. His eyes were as deep blue as the sky outside, his hair must originally have been blonde but was now bleached to nearly white by the sun. He smiled and nodded.

'That's Lynn Hanson,' Victoria said. 'Lynn dear, this is Carver Ellis.'

The young man nodded in my direction.

'Besides being a ravaging appetite on two legs,' Victoria continued, 'he is also the best all-around handyman in the valley. I couldn't make it any more without him doing all the heavy chores. He's been chopping firewood for winter.'

I might have guessed that much. It certainly explained the axe he had been carrying when I saw him briefly some time earlier. And it also explained the sheen of perspiration on his skin. He had his shirt off when he came in, but as soon as he saw me he pulled it over his head, ruffling his hair even more and giving himself — all unknowing, I'm sure — an intriguingly outdoorsy look.

He was deeply tanned, with smoothly muscled shoulders and arms, and a narrow waist and flat stomach that spoke volumes for either a rigorous training program or an active life outside.

Given the circumstances, I opted for the latter.

He grinned at me, rather shyly I thought, but all the more appealingly for that. And as I extended my hand and shook his, noticing his thick calluses and the strength of his fingers, it struck me that he was an enormously attractive man who had no idea the kind of impression he must make on every impressionable young thing for miles around.

Young thing? Or old thing, for that matter. Even I — old has-been that I am at twenty-nine — felt flustered when he grinned and caught my eyes with his.

'Miz Hanson,' he said, carefully letting his pronunciation fall midway between *Mrs.* and *Miss* in the way so many people did in the area.

'*Mrs.*' I said. Then: 'My husband . . . died . . . a while ago.'

There might have been a flickering moment of disappointment at the *Mrs.*, followed by the slightest increase in interest in my current marital status, but if he intended to say anything about it, he never got the chance.

'Miz Sears!'

The voice was sharp, a high treble fraught with anxiety. It burst from somewhere outside the house.

She jerked around from the sink where she was still working on lunch, her cheeks suddenly pale, and ran from the room, faster than I would have expected a woman half her age to move.

'What . . . ' I began, but Carver was also already on the move.

I followed him through the living room and on out to the front yard.

'Something must be wicked wrong,' he shouted over his shoulder. 'She can always tell.'

Victoria was beyond the picket fence and running full-tilt toward the trailhead at the end of the road.

'Miz Sears!'

This time I could see the boy, half sliding, half falling down the last slope between the thickest pines and the road. It was one of the boys from that morning, obviously, but his pack was gone and his hair was spiky, like it had been wet and he had come away without combing it. His T-shirt was filthy with sweat and dust, and there was a long rip in the knee of his jeans. As he got closer, I could see blood on the material and could tell that the boy was limping in spite of his efforts to keep running.

'Miz Sears!' he screamed again, his voice breaking.

'Toby, what's wrong!' she yelled in response.

By that time, Carver had outpaced her and approached the boy. He towered over the youngster, and without any apparent effort reached down and picked the boy up and carried him back toward the house.

The boy — Toby — was panting and breathless, and beneath the dirt on his face I saw a pallor of fear and terror that immediately caught at my heart. Bloodless face, bloody knee, hands shaking from the strain, he struggled to find the breath to speak.

'Alix, Miz Sears . . . , Alix . . . at the pool . . . '

'Yes, Toby, go on,' Victoria said patiently, but I could hear undertones of concern in her voice. Carver's arms suddenly began to tremble, as if Toby's weight were too much for him, although the musculature in his shoulders seemed to contradict that.

'What about Alix?' Carver asked in a rough voice.

'Alix . . . , 'the boy began, as if he were afraid to continue, afraid of what he would have to say. He closed his eyes and began to cry. 'Alix is dead.'

3

Under Victoria's direction, Carver carried the exhausted boy back into the house and seated him in a deep armchair in the living room.

As he straightened, Victoria said, 'Now you run on up there, Carver. Find out what's going on and what's needed. I'll call the deputy station from here. Wroten or Allen will probably be here by the time you all get back. If not I'll send them on up.'

Carver was already out the door and running across the front yard. He probably didn't even hear the screen door slam.

'Now, young man, let's take care of you,' she said to the trembling figure in the chair.

'But Miz Sears . . . '

'No buts. There's nothing we can do 'til we find out what's happened for sure. Neither up at the falls nor down in the village. So let's get you settled.'

She swept out of the room, leaving me with the boy.

He was older than Shawn had been — perhaps twelve to Shawn's six — but he seemed to resemble Shawn in frightening ways. His longish dark hair was unkempt and dusty at the moment, but even in the best of circumstances it would probably look as if it had never been combed. He was deeply tanned from the summer sun, with dark brown eyes.

Shawn's eyes had been blue. But given an additional five or six years, he might have . . .

'Here we are,' Victoria said. It was as if she burst into the room, all energy and vitality, even though she made almost no noise. She carried a tray with a steaming mug and what looked like a sandwich. 'Just drink this first. Then take a few bites.'

She held out the mug.

The boy — Toby — looked as if he were about to refuse, or at least put up a bit of an argument, but finally grabbed the cup, holding it gingerly with both

43

hands, and took a tentative sip.

'Hot,' he said softly.

Victoria nodded. 'Chamomile tea,' she explained to me. 'Very relaxing.'

We waited for a few minutes while Toby caught his breath, then Victoria pulled a straight-back chair up close to his, caught one of his hands in hers, and said, 'Now, dear. Tell us about it.'

He looked at her, almost for reassurance, then began. 'We had just got to our camping spot. You know, the big, flat space just the beyond the falls, where the creek is still pretty slow and there's some good fishing sometimes.'

Victoria nodded.

'Anyway, some of us were starting to set up our stuff and some of the others wandered over to the falls, you know, to mess around on the rocks. Mr. Mintern yelled at them to be careful.'

He stopped for a moment before continuing, 'I mean, we all know the rocks can be dangerous and everything, and Mr. Mintern's pretty careful about . . . '

'I'm sure he is, Toby. What happened then?'

'Well, we saw where some people had been eating, you know, like having a picnic. There was a little fire pit and some bits of paper scattered around, you know, like you would wrap hiking food in, sandwiches and stuff. Like that.'

'More than enough for one person?'

'I think so. Anyway, there was a mess-kit there as well. The pot had been sitting on the fire but all of the water had boiled away and what was left inside was pretty much charred. And a couple of metal cups. The stuff was Dale's.'

I must have looked curious because Toby looked at me as he explained.

'Alix's little brother, Dale. He's a friend of mine. It was his mess-kit up there.'

'You're sure about that, Toby?' Victoria seemed slightly surprised at his words.

'Yeah. The pot has a little dent in it from last time we were camping. Some of us had put an old cow patty in it and he was really pissed at us. He knocked the pot against a rock to get the shi . . . the stuff out. He must have boiled five gallons of water to make sure it was clean. Boy, was he mad. But he got back at us. He . . .'

'I'm sure he did,' Victoria interrupted. 'Dale wasn't with you, today, though, was he?'

Toby looked startled, then a pained expression flitted across his face.

'I never thought of that,' he said breathlessly. 'No, Dale told me yesterday that he couldn't come. He got grounded 'cause of . . . '

'No need to tattle on what he did, now is there, Toby?'

'No, Miz Sears. But anyway, he couldn't come today. I'm awful glad he wasn't there.'

Victoria seemed satisfied with her progress thus far, so she paused for a moment, then continued. I noticed that by now, the boy seemed much more self-possessed, as if talking about the mundane details of what they had found at the camping site had calmed him, made it easier to face what was obviously coming next.

'Now, Toby, what happened then?'

'Well, one of the older guys — I'm not sure which one it was — but one of them yelled, 'Hey, I think there's someone down there! In the pond!' The others

46

climbed out onto the rock he was standing on and looked down as well, then they all started coming back toward the creek bank, yelling.

'By then, Mr. Mintern was closer, and they said something about seeing a body or something at the bottom of the falls, so he yelled back at us to stay put and he and the older guys started climbing down the rocks along the falls.

'It took them a long time. You know how wet and slippery those rock are.'

Victoria nodded but said nothing.

'Anyway, after a while, one of the bigger guys — Rob, it was, you know Rob, don't you? — anyway, he came climbing back up the rocks and ran across to where the rest of us were standing.

'"Who's the fastest runner here?' he yelled. Everybody pointed at me, and Rob says, 'Okay, you get the hell down to Miz Sears' place, fast as you can.''

Toby had flushed heavily and carefully avoided looking at me.

'Sorry for the language, ma'am, but that's what Rob said.'

'It's quite all right,' I said, feeling both

foolish and a bit in awe of the boy who had been so close to where death had struck and still found it in himself to worry about some stranger's sensitivities.

'Anyway,' Toby continued, 'Rob said, 'Alix Macrorie's dead, and you need to have Miz Sears call the cops and tell them to get out here.'

'I didn't believe him at first and just stood there, but he took a swipe at my a . . . at my butt and yelled, 'Get going!' so I took off. When I got down the path a ways, past the falls, I could see a bunch of the older guys and Mr. Mintern standing around the edge of the water, but I didn't stop. I just ran like . . . ran as fast as I could down here.

'I tripped a couple of times and went down, but I got right back up and kept going.

'Then Carver met me outside the fence and caught me just before I fell again. Man, I've never been so tired.'

The boy leaned back against the back of the armchair and took a sip of the tea. It was probably cold by now, but he didn't complain.

Victoria stood and walked over to the front door, still open from when Carver had rushed out. She seemed to be thinking, or staring at something.

Far away, I thought I could hear a siren approaching and was about to mention it when Victoria turned.

'That will be the deputies from the station in Fox Creek. I phoned them while I was in the kitchen. Doc Anderson should be with them. He's the local doctor . . . and what passes for a coroner in such a sparsely populated area.'

Sure enough, not half a minute later, flashes of red alternating with blue flickered through the windows and the front door. Victoria stepped out.

'You wait here, Toby. Why don't you keep him company, Lynn dear?'

She was gone before I could answer.

The boy and I sat in uncomfortable silence for several minutes before Victoria returned. She stamped her feet before entering, raising a small cloud of dust on the porch. She had apparently gone as far as the dirt trail leading, I supposed, up to the falls.

49

'Deputy Wroten came. And Doc. They're on their way to the falls. Doc brought a couple of other men, in case they needed help with the . . . any help,' she finished weakly, glancing at Toby. 'Deputy Wroten asked if you two would please stay here with me until he returns. Will that be all right, Lynn dear?'

I nodded.

Victoria led Toby into a back room and returned a few minutes later.

'He's laying down now. I must confess that I put a bit of something extra in the chamomile, something to help him get some sleep. He's probably too upset to rest on his own, but he has to be exhausted from running all that way. He'll need to be able to repeat his story for the authorities when they return.

'It's too dark and stuffy in here,' she added, although the room was bright with midday sun and a soft breeze was fluttering the drapes at the windows. 'Let's go outside for a while and wait there.'

It was bright in the open air but the floppy hat provided welcome shade.

Victoria and I wandered through her garden again, then walked a short way up the trailhead leading to the falls. She kept glancing at the ground as if she were looking for something but didn't say what. Most of the time she simply chattered on in a soft, soothing voice, pointing out trees and plants and different kinds of rocks along the way. I got the feeling that she was trying to keep my mind occupied . . . away from thoughts of death.

Surprisingly, it worked. I silently thanked her for that.

After a while, we returned to the meadow and were about to go into the house when an odd sound attracted our attention.

Behind the house, a dirt road cut off at almost right angles from the trail, crossed the upper edge of the meadow, and disappeared into the thick trees. Somewhere further up the road, an engine roared now and again, as if the vehicle it was powering kept getting momentarily stuck in ruts and needed an extra bit of *umph* to get out.

'That would be Lance. Mr. Prescott,' Victoria said, taking my arm and leading me back toward the rough road.

A few seconds later, a new but extremely mud-caked Jeep made its way through the furrows and potholes, canting once on a large rock that caught it just under one tire. We watched it approach until it drew even with us. The driver cut the engine and jumped out.

He was older than Carver Ellis by a few years, perhaps a year or two younger than me, tall, dressed in clothes that were just as dusty as the Jeep but looked somehow new and even slightly awkward on him. He gave Victoria a hug and turned to shake hands with me.

'Lynn dear, this is Lance Prescott. Lance, this is Lynn Hanson. She's staying at the van Etten place just down the road.'

'Pleased, ma'am.' His voice was a pleasant baritone with perhaps just a touch too much of the Western drawl in the final word. I remembered Victoria's earlier description of the man and stifled a laugh.

'I was on my way down to the village to

pick up some things. Something going on here?' He motioned toward the vehicles parked at the end of Victoria's driveway. 'Lots of cars there.'

'There's been . . . an accident. At the falls. A girl from Fox Creek has apparently been killed. The deputy and Doc Anderson are up there now.'

'How did she die?' Prescott seemed shaken — his voice had a tremulous note to it. He was young enough still that a sudden confrontation with death — even if vicariously — might be alarming.

'I don't know yet. All I know is that some Scouts went up there with Roy Mintern and one of them saw a body at the bottom of the falls.'

'Who . . . who was it?'

'Alexandra Macrorie. Alix. She worked at the cafe. Maybe you knew her?' Victoria watched the man's face closely as she spoke. I got the impression that the question was important to her.

'No. No, I don't think so. I don't know many of the people down there.' He suddenly turned a thousand-watt smile toward Victoria. 'And anyway, no one around here could compete with my best girl.' He lifted her and whirled her around, laughing. She giggled like a schoolgirl.

'Now, Lance. You put me down this instant. This isn't seemly.'

He carefully set her on her feet. She patted her hair.

'Young Mr. Prescott can be a terrible flirt, Lynn dear. You had best be careful around him.'

I felt myself blushing and would have tried to respond but just then Victoria turned to face the trail to the falls and said, 'Here comes Roy with the boys.'

A few minutes later, we had formed a small cluster near his van, outside the front of the house.

'Don't know much more than that, Miz Sears,' Mintern said stolidly as he slid the van door closed. The boys — including Toby, who had emerged from the house at Victoria's call, looking sleepy and slightly confused — were inside, sitting more quietly than seemed natural. That was to be expected, I suppose. The deputy had sent word that Toby would not need to wait since he hadn't really seen anything of particular relevance, and Mintern was taking the group back to town where, undoubtedly, worried parents were waiting for them. The news of the girl's death had probably spread by now, given what little I knew of small-town grapevines.

'Wroten and the others will be down in a while with the body' — he glanced at the door, making sure that it was tightly closed — 'after Doc's had a chance to look at it. All I can say is that she looked really battered, shattered, like she had fallen from the top of the falls and struck every sharp rock on the way down. Her face was cut up bad. Probably had a lot of broken bones, as well.'

'She was . . . clothed?' Victoria asked quietly.

Mintern nodded. 'Yeah. Looked like she was dressed for hiking. Boots, jeans. Blouse was ripped here and there, though. Jeans torn a little. Probably from the fall.'

Victoria nodded but said no more.

'I told Wroten everything I knew, being

in charge of the boys, you know, and being there when she was . . . found.'

Victoria laid a hand on his arm, a gesture replete with sympathy and concern.

'He told me to keep myself handy, in case he had any more questions. Said he might want to talk to me some more tomorrow, after he asks around and finds out more about Alix . . . who knew her, who her friends were, that sort of thing. It almost sounded like he thought I might have had something to do with . . . what happened.' At this, he sounded more miserable than before, as if the fact of death had abruptly become more personal.

'I'm sure it's just a formality, Roy.' Victoria gave his arm a quick squeeze of reassurance. 'Nothing to worry about. Just tell him everything he wants to know.'

'Well, I better get this bunch on the road,' Mintern said a moment or two later as he climbed into the van. 'Thanks for your help, Miz Sears. And for taking care of Toby.'

'Don't mention it, Roy. Drive carefully.'

Mintern glanced at Prescott and me. 'Mrs. Hanson. Mr. Prescott.' We each gave a small wave in return, then the van backed out of the drive, made a three-point turn, and disappeared in the direction of Fox Creek.

'Curious,' Victoria murmured.

I didn't know what to say, and apparently neither did Prescott, so we merely followed her back into the house.

I had expected the same kind of easy chat from her that we had shared earlier that afternoon but, after a quick, piercing look at Prescott — which he pointedly did not return — she picked up her knitting and began work.

Prescott and I started to make small-talk once or twice, but Victoria's silence and the general atmosphere of the day quickly stifled each attempt. Finally we all simply sat there, each wrapped in our own thoughts.

Mine were not pleasant.

It must have been an hour later — getting on toward three or four o'clock, when we heard the first noises outside. Victoria rose quickly, as if she had been forewarned, and disappeared through the door. We heard her calling out to the approaching men.

Prescott and I remained sitting, feeling more than slightly uncomfortable, I assume, since neither of us were really part of the community, nor did we know anything about the accident, or the victim. Eventually, though, we rose as well and walked outside.

Three men were just sliding a covered stretcher into the back of a van — the coroner's, apparently — while a man in uniform and another man I recognized as Carver were speaking to Victoria. The three men climbed into the van, and after a few words with the man in the uniform, the driver half-saluted and drove off.

Prescott and I were midway to the small knot of people when Carver looked up, saw Prescott, and bellowed, 'You bastard! I'm going to kill . . . '

He lunged toward us, but the man in the uniform — Deputy Wroten, as it turned out — was just as fast and grabbed Carver's arm, yanking him back. Victoria stepped in front of Carver, her hand on his chest, even though she was so tiny that if he had wanted to he could have bowled her right over.

At my side, Prescott stopped cold. When I looked at him, his face was white beneath his tan — and the slight edge of dust that still clung to him. His lips were compressed tightly and I could see the muscles in his jaw working convulsively.

Something was going on, and I had no idea what.

'You bastard!' Carver yelled. 'Let me go!' — this to the deputy, who made no movement to do as he had been ordered. 'Let me get my hands . . . '

Wroten and Victoria both spoke urgently to Carver, although I could not hear their words. Prescott remained stock-still, stone-like except for the movement of his jaws and his heavy breathing.

Carver finally seemed to respond to whatever Wroten was saying — threats or promises, I don't know which — because Wroten let go and, with Victoria's arm linked lightly through his, Carver began a slow, almost stumbling shamble toward the house.

Prescott whirled and started toward his Jeep.

'Mr. Prescott,' Wroten said, forcefully

but not particularly loudly, 'I would appreciate it if you would join us in the house.'

Prescott paused, one foot half-off the ground, as if he were not certain which way to proceed, then whirled, walked back toward the house and disappeared inside.

I started to head toward the road, fully intending to return to the peace and quite of the van Etten's cabin. After all, I had nothing to do with any of this. I had known none of these people for longer than a few hours, and certainly had never even met the victim. I had enough to think about today, anyway. I simply did not want to get involved.

But by then, Victoria was standing next to me and linked her free arm in mine and said, as sweetly as if she were inviting me to a Sunday-after-church brunch, 'You'll stay for supper, won't you, Lynn dear. I wouldn't think of letting you walk all that way back to your place without something to eat.'

'Ma'am,' Wroten began, 'Miz Sears, I don't think . . . '

'Then perhaps you shouldn't, should you?' she answered, just as sweetly.

4

'You sit here, Ellis,' Wroten said peremptorily, nearly pushing Carver into a nearby chair. 'And you can sit there, Mr. Prescott, if you would,' motioning to one directly across the living room. Apparently Victoria and I were free to sit anywhere we wished, so we did.

Victoria crossed the room, switching on several lamps as she did so. Outside, the day was bright and clear, but in the early afternoon the house was partly in shade. The lamps cast sharp shadows around the room. She took her usual place and carefully arranged her knitting on her lap. I sat next to her. Wroten remained standing.

'Here's the way I see things,' he began. 'This is what we *know*. We have a girl dead. Now, chances are that she fell to her death. Doc Anderson says that based on what he could see up there, she has been dead since late yesterday, and she probably didn't drown. He's going to give me an official report on that tomorrow morning.

'So she could have been climbing around on the rocks at the top of the Falls, hit a slick one, and lost her footing. Doc says that falling from that height might — I say *might* — account for her injuries. Again, he will know more about that tomorrow.'

Victoria had taken up her knitting and begun working the needles, softly *click*-ing and *clack*-ing a faint counterpoint to Wroten's words. He seemed not to have noticed. Thus far, all of his attention was divided between Carver and Prescott. They, in turn, were acting subdued, sullen, refusing to meet anyone's eyes.

To my untrained mind, they both looked guilty . . . of something.

'Now for what we *don't* know.

'Doc has said 'maybe' to a lot of things, but can't be certain until he examines the body more closely. He's probably starting that right now. If need be, we can send the body down-mountain for a full autopsy. That will take time. So for now, we don't know for certain whether Alix Macrorie drowned, whether she fell accidentally, whether she might have been pushed, or whether she was beaten to death first and then dumped over the Falls.'

At this both Carver and Prescott leaped to their feet, angry and yelling, although in the turmoil I couldn't follow their words.

'Down, you two!' Wroten ordered.

'Now, Deputy Wroten, I'm sure there's no need to shout,' Victoria said. 'These two boys will sit right down and behave themselves, won't you?' There was something icy beneath the gentility of her voice, and to my astonishment both Carver and Prescott dropped silently back into their seats.

'That's better. Please continue.'

'Right. Uh . . . in addition, Doc says it is unlikely in the extreme that if the body had fallen from the rocks along the side of the Falls it would have landed where it was. Almost the only way for it to have been half-in the pool like that would be if it had arced at some point into the

Falls . . . thus, Alix was probably — *probably* — either pushed or thrown.'

He paused to stare at the men, as if daring them to start arguing again. Neither spoke. Neither moved.

'All right. Point two: there were at least two people at the top of the falls yesterday. What little evidence we have strongly supports that assumption. All of the scouts — and Roy Mintern — agree that when they arrived at the camp site, they found the remains of a fire, long since burned out, part of a mess-kit, and *two* cups. Both had some liquid left in the bottom, but unfortunately, we will never know what it was.

'Like the eager-beaver Scouts they are, the whole group set about policing the area before they set up their own camp, before the body was discovered. They tossed whatever had been in the pot — some kind of leaves for a tea, most likely, from what they reported to me — into the creek and thoroughly washed the entire mess-kit. Apparently it belonged to one of their friends who couldn't go on the camp-out.'

'That would be little Dale Macrorie, Alix's brother,' Victoria said. 'Toby recognized the pot by a . . . uh, a distinguishing mark.'

'Did he? None of the others said anything about it belonging to Alix's brother. Just that it was a friend's and they were doing a good deed.'

'I would suppose that after Alix . . . after the body was found, they were too stunned to tell you. It took Toby a while to get to that point when we talked about things earlier today.'

Wroten shook his head. 'Might have known you wouldn't just let the kid rest.'

'Yes, you might have.'

I felt like I was watching a verbal tennis match for a moment, one then the other, back and forth. Wroten kept his temper well — I'm not sure I would have taken someone like Victoria interfering with my case like that had I been the investigating officer in charge, and I know that the L.A. police would have looked with great disfavor at Victoria's questioning a witness, even a peripheral one, before the case had been resolved. After the accident last year . . .

But Wroten was talking again.

'Okay. So the mess-kit belonged to Dale Macrorie. Alix must have taken it for the day. I'll check with the boy on that.

'But in addition to the mess-kit, we were able to find a couple of things in the litter the Scouts collected to indicate that at least two people were present. Alix being one of them.

'And that leads to point number three. Apparently, it would have been highly unlike her for Alix Macrorie to have gone hiking or on a camping trip . . . with *anyone*. From what I was able to glean from the older scouts and Roy Mintern, she was usually distinctly uncomfortable in the wild. She rarely left town. She had her job there, she had her friends there — none of them particularly outdoorsy types — none of the guys at the scene today could think of a reason why she would have *willingly* gone up to the falls. With anyone. Yet obviously, she did.'

Victoria continued her knitting. 'Point four?' she asked, as if she knew what was coming.

'Point four. The troop pretty much destroyed most of the tracks that might have existed of anyone coming up the trail to the Falls.'

Victoria nodded. I remembered us walking part way along the dirt path earlier that afternoon. It had seemed like she was looking for something. Tracks? Whatever she was looking for, she hadn't seemed to have found it, yet neither had she seemed upset or disappointed.

'What that tells us is . . . '

'What that tells you is that *no one* — including Alix Macrorie — went up that path yesterday,' Victoria announced, finally dropping her knitting back into her lap. 'I could have told you that.'

It was as if she had dropped a bombshell. For the moment, everyone was watching her — Wroten, caught in mid-sentence. Carver, face screwed up in some strong emotion, anger or frustration, or . . . I don't know what. And Prescott, still white, lips compressed as if to keep any stray sounds from escaping.

'I suppose,' Victoria said almost primly, 'that if this were a novel or a movie, I should surge to my feet, point to the murderer, and announce, *'J'accuse!'* Or at the very least, the lights should go out, a shot should ring through the darkness, and then when the lights returned, we would discover that the butler did it. Or that I had been shot dead.'

No one spoke. I think we were all a bit stunned that she would try to break into the seriousness of the situation with levity.

I suppose also that none of us really knew Victoria Sears as well as we might have thought.

'How . . . ?' Wroten began.

'Because I didn't hear anyone. If anyone — by car, on horseback, or on foot — had gone up that trail yesterday, believe me, I would have known.'

Strangely, perhaps, we all believed her.

At least no one tried to argue the point with her.

'Therefore,' she continued, 'they — Alix and her companion or companions — hiked to the Falls another way. And unless she was willing to trail-blaze through some almost impossibly thick stands of pine and fir, thorns and brush, there is only one other accessible way to get close to Porcupine Falls.'

Here she turned to study Prescott.

'And that is the track that passes directly in front of the line cabin. It cuts off from the county road about a mile above town — not too far, actually, from where the Ellises live, come to think of it — then angles up into my property just to the north of here. It dead ends a few hundred yards beyond the cabin. Where you are staying, Lance.'

Prescott started to rise, then apparently thought better of it, and sank back down.

'I didn't see . . . anyone . . . yesterday.' He almost mumbled his words. I had some difficulty understanding what he was saying. It was as if he felt he had to respond but didn't want to draw attention to himself.

Victoria simply kept watching him, as if he were an unusual, perhaps unique specimen under her own private microscope.

'I didn't,' he repeated. 'I was . . . I was away from the cabin almost all day. Back in the woods, exploring in the other direction. Away from the falls. I didn't see anyone.'

'Very well,' Victoria said, after a long pause. 'Very well.'

'So what you're telling me is that basically we have two viable possibilities for this mysterious companion . . . ,' Wroten began.

' . . . Or companions.'

'Sitting right in this room,' Wroten continued. 'Two young men who could conceivably have accompanied Alix Mac-rorie to the Falls without having passed by your place, Miz Sears.'

'That's correct. Of course, any number of other people might have been with Alix yesterday. The track isn't exactly a secret, you know, and I have never tried to keep people from hiking in. In fact, as you can tell from the presence of the scouts today, the Porcupine Falls is quite a popular place.

'Usually, though, people heading there have the . . . shall we say, the *courtesy* to drop by and say hello on their way.'

Wroten stood silently for a few

moments, his face suggesting that a number of thoughts were passing rapidly through his mind.

'So the next question would be, how well did the two of you know Alix Macrorie? Prescott, what about you?'

'Mrs. Sears can tell you that I almost never go to Fox Creek, maybe only once a week or so.'

'I'm sure she can. But that isn't what I asked. Did you know Alix Macrorie?'

'I don't think so. I don't even know what she looks . . . looked like. Maybe I passed her on the street or saw her at the store or something, but I never . . . '

'No!' Carver actually was on his feet again, shouting and pointing. 'No! It must have been him! He must have been with her yesterday! And killed her! That's the only . . . '

Wroten turned to push Carver back toward the chair.

'That's enough from you,' he started to say, but Carver swatted at Wroten's hand and knocked it out of his way. He took another furious step toward Prescott. 'No! It's not true, that he didn't know her. I saw them together. Day before yesterday. In town. He was . . . '

'Carver, that's it. Sit down!' Wroten brought up his hand again to restrain the younger man, but Carver had apparently had enough. He swung again, no half-hearted batting motion but rather a full-fledged from-the-shoulder swing that caught the deputy square on the chin.

Caught by surprise, Wroten went down and stayed down and didn't move again, but Carver didn't stop there. He nearly leaped the distance across the living room and threw himself on Prescott, already swinging away.

But Prescott was a young man, too, and for all that he lacked Carver's bulk, he was strong and quick. He darted out of his chair sideways, but in doing so he clipped the edge of Victoria's armchair and upended it.

With a sharp yelp of shock, she went over, striking her head obliquely on the end table next to her and knocking an antique brass-based lamp onto the floor. With a vicious crash and a loud crackling sound, the light went out, and a second later so did all of the rest of the lights in the room.

It wasn't exactly the pitch blackness Victoria had brought to mind with her reference to fictional murders, but the abrupt shift from bright to dim was startling and for a moment I felt as if I had been blinded. It was shadowy enough for me to lose sight of exactly what was happening.

I jumped up and started to reach for Victoria, but someone bumped into me with enough force to knock me to the floor. I fell, trying to brace myself with my hands. With a sharp *crack* something seemed to give way in my wrist. I screamed — as much in startlement as in a sudden rush of pain — and then for an instant everything truly did go black.

There was a moment of absolute silence. Then a scrabbling sound like someone struggling to regain his footing. And almost instantly thereafter, the thudding of running feet. A moment later the screen clattered and I roused sufficiently to see Carver race outside and disappear into the surrounding forest.

I fell back against the floor, cradling my arm and moaning.

It seemed as if an infinity passed.

'Lynn dear,' Victoria said in what was very nearly a whisper.

It was perhaps only five minutes later.

I was stretched out on the couch. Prescott had apparently lurched to his feet only moments after Carver had fled and rushed to help me. Victoria was on her feet by then as well, shaken, with a bit of a bruise on her temple, but basically unhurt. Wroten had begun to groan from across the room but still had made no movement to rise.

Between them, Victoria and Prescott had gotten me settled, then Victoria disappeared into the kitchen. She returned bearing a small first-aid kit.

'I'm not a Boy Scout,' she said soothingly, 'but I'm always prepared.'

Prescott looked on as she settled beside me and, taking my injured wrist, gently felt along tendons and bones, pressing here and there just hard enough to feel the resistance she apparently hoped to feel. It hurt, but never as badly as it had during the first few moments.

'I think you've a sprained wrist, dear. We'll have Doc Anderson check it as soon as we can, but I really can't feel anything broken.'

She disappeared into the kitchen again and this time returned with a small bag of frozen peas. 'Twenty minutes of cold, every three or four hours. We'll see how that works. And take these.'

She handed me two small pills.

'Ibuprofen,' she said with a smile. 'Store-bought. I'm afraid it doesn't grow in my front yard.'

I tried to laugh but the sound caught in my throat.

'Lance dear, perhaps you had better see to Deputy Wroten. He's having difficulty getting up, I believe.'

With a scowl on his face, Prescott walked over — none too briskly, it seemed — and offered Wroten a grudging hand. It took the deputy a couple of tries before he was on his feet, shaking his head groggily and rubbing his jaw. A long deep bruise was already visible along the angle of the bone.

He steadied himself with a chair, then crossed the room to stand by Victoria.

'Is she all right?'

'Oh, yes. I think so. Just a bit of a sprain. Here' — she held out two more of the small pills — 'I suspect you could probably use some of these yourself.'

He glared at the pills, shook his head . . . and groaned softly. He took the pills and dry-swallowed them. The thought of doing that made me slightly nauseated. I could almost feel the acrid taste in my own mouth.

'I think everyone should sit down for a bit,' Victoria said. 'Things seem to have taken a rather surprising turn. I would never have expected such behavior from Carver. Unless . . . '

'Unless what?'

'Oh, nothing important. Just a random thought. Probably not relevant.'

Wroten waited as if to give her time to answer more fully. When she didn't, he asked, 'May I use your telephone, Miz Sears?'

'In the kitchen.'

He disappeared into the other room.

Prescott glanced toward the open front door.

'You'd better not, Lance. I think it would be by far wiser for you to wait this out. At least until Deputy Wroten has a chance to talk with you. Carver has already made himself seem unduly suspicious by his actions. There is no need for you to do the same thing. Is there?'

'No. No, ma'am.'

From the kitchen, Wroten's voice droned on for a couple of minutes. I could hear the intonations but not the words. He seemed angry, but then I would have been angry if I had just been knocked cold by a man who might — just might — have cold-bloodedly attacked and murdered a young woman the day before.

None of us spoke further. My wrist throbbed but I found that I could move my fingers easily enough. Nothing seemed broken. The ice-pack must have been helping.

When Wroten returned, Victoria did not say anything, but he answered the questions obvious in her expression.

'I've asked Allen — Ewert Allen, my

deputy — to get together a couple of volunteers and start checking around to see if they can locate Ellis. Check his home, friends, that sort of thing.'

'Carver lives with his mother, she's been widowed since he was a boy, and he really doesn't have that many friends,' Victoria said. 'Perhaps . . . '

'Well, they will keep an eye out around town for him. But in the meantime, I do have a couple of questions for our other . . . person of interest here.'

Prescott interlaced his hands together and stared down at them.

'I'm going to start from the assumption that you might not have had anything to do with the Macrorie girl's death. You could have run away, like Ellis did, but you're still here. And you didn't take a swing at me. From that I figure that you might not be involved. *Might* not. Now convince me.

'Can you see Porcupine Falls from the line cabin?'

'It's a couple of miles away, but the cabin is on a ridge overlooking the valley and Redbud Creek. It's quite a nice view, actually, which is one reason . . . '

'I'm sure it is,' Wroten said. 'But I'm more interested in whether you saw anything along the Creek yesterday.'

'Maybe I could have, if I'd had my binoculars and was looking that way, but like I said earlier, I was out exploring yesterday. In the opposite direction. Further up the mountains. I was looking for . . . uh, for signs of wildlife, birds, that sort of thing. It was a nice day. Too nice to stay around the cabin.'

'Did you know Alix Macrorie?'

'Like I said, I don't get to town much. I might have seen her in passing without knowing it.'

'Didn't Alix work at the café?' Victoria spoke into the brief silence.

'Yeah,' Wroten said. 'Most days, with occasional evenings, according to Mintern. He said he ate there quite a bit — apparently Mrs. Mintern isn't the world's greatest cook so he doesn't go home for lunch very often — and knew her in passing.'

'I though you said you'd been to the café a couple of times, Lance.'

'Uh . . . yeah, yeah I have. Maybe I saw her there, if she was a waitress or something. I don't know.'

'Excuse me for a moment,' Victoria said, rising and moving silently into the kitchen. I heard her speaking, apparently on the telephone, but she kept her voice low so I don't think any of us knew who she was calling.'

'Effie Pettingill,' Victoria said as she re-entered the living room, answering the question no one had asked. 'If anything is happening in Fox Creek, Effie knows about it. I'm not sure how, since she almost never leaves her house, but she does.

'She says that Alix has been working at the Good Eats since she graduated from high school last year. There aren't that many jobs for young people in Fox Creek, so Alix was lucky. She was pretty regular, didn't miss work very often and when she did, she always had good reasons. Yesterday would have been her day off.'

'Does Effie Pettingill know who killed her?' Wroten asked, only in part sarcastically.

'Of course not,' Victoria said. 'If she did, she would have told me right away. I think. Though Effie does like to hold on to her secrets sometimes.

'She did, however, say that Carver has been, as she put it, 'panting around Good Eats with his tongue hanging out like a hound-dog in heat' more frequently than usual. Especially later in the day, toward the end of Alix's shifts. He's our version of a *johannes factotum*, Lynn, our jack-of-all-trades handyman, so he can pretty much set his own schedule.'

'So maybe *he* knows . . . knew her,' Prescott said, rising again and starting to pace. 'Maybe *he* took her out to the falls, maybe they had an argument and he pushed her. Maybe he was afraid that you'd figure things out and that's why he cold-cocked you and bolted.'

Wroten didn't look too happy with the way the younger man had described the brief altercation, but he didn't say anything about that. Instead: 'Maybe. I'll do some checking when I get back to town. In the meantime, Mr. Prescott, I think you had best get yourself back up to your cabin and stay there. Get a good night's sleep, because I will expect you to present yourself at the station tomorrow at 9:00 sharp. I'll have some further questions for you, and by then I'm pretty sure we'll have Mr. Ellis as well. Then we'll settle a few things among us.'

I wondered what made Wroten think that Prescott wouldn't, as he had phrased it, *bolt* as well if he did in fact have any secrets he wanted to keep, but Victoria didn't appear to have any qualms about Wroten's decision.

'He'll be there, deputy, don't worry. I know him. I know him better than he thinks. He won't try to run away.'

With those rather cryptic remarks, she motioned for Prescott to leave.

'Drop by for breakfast before you go into town, Lance, will you? You must be getting pretty tired of field rations by now.'

'Not really . . . well, actually, breakfast sounds great, Mrs. Sears. See you then. Good night, Mrs. Hanson.' He made as if to tip an invisible hat to me. 'See you at 9:00, Deputy Wroten.'

With that he left.

Wroten dropped into the nearest chair and again groaned softly.

'Headache?'

'A little. But mostly I'm just frustrated. Do you mind if I wait here for a bit. I've told Allen to call me here if he finds out anything. To be honest, I could do with a bit of a rest.'

'Of course, you're welcome to stay. But I don't think that would be wise right now.' Victoria rose and retrieved something from her first-aid kit — an Ace bandage, as it proved — and returned to sit by me. As she began to wrap my wrist, she said, 'Whenever you have a sprain, Lynn dear, always remember R.I.C.E.'

The sudden irrelevance startled me. What did *rice* have to do with anything.

'R-I-C-E. Rest — Ice — Compression — Elevation. The best treatment. As soon as I've finished wrapping this, we'll get a snug sling on you to elevate it. Then we can all take a nice, leisurely walk to relax.'

'Walk?' Wroten seemed as nonplussed as I felt.

'Walk. I think it will do Lynn good — it

won't be anything too vigorous, dear, considering your injury — and, since you've become entangled in this mess, I think you will want to be there with us.'

'Where?'

'To talk to Carver Ellis. I think I know where he will be.'

5

We set out twenty minutes later. Victoria had taken the time to change into outdoor clothing — she said what I was wearing would be appropriate for me — and put a small band-aid over the bruise on her forehead where she had struck her head on the end table. It had begun to show a bead or two of blood.

'This?' she had scoffed when Wroten asked her if she was up to going anywhere. 'This little bump? Nothing at all. I've had worse hangnails.'

I couldn't imagine Victoria Sears with anything quite so plebian as a hangnail but decided not to mention that.

Nor would she say anything more when Wroten tried to question her about where she was taking us.

'You'll know soon enough. Let an old woman have a moment of drama, for heaven's sake.'

He tried to convince her that Carver's

location was a police matter, that if she knew where the young man was she should tell him immediately so he could call in back up — after all, technically Carver was clearly guilty of assault on an officer of the law, in front of three witnesses, no less, regardless of whether or not he could be implicated in the death of Alix Macrorie, and therefore he was to be considered at least potentially dangerous.

'Nonsense,' she had said lightly. 'That boy would not hurt a mosquito that he caught in the process of drinking his blood.'

I didn't know Carver as well as Victoria did — I had only met him hours before, although so much had happened that it seemed much longer than that — but I wasn't so sure he was harmless. I remembered the way I had first seen him, a powerfully muscled young man, impulsive, swinging an axe as easily as if it were a fly-swatter as he raced around the corner of the house. It didn't take much imagination to transform that image into one of a madman hell-bent on homicide.

Mentally I excused myself to Victoria for the language. Toby seemed to have rubbed off on me.

Wroten seemed to trust Victoria at her word, at least far enough that he didn't call for back up. He did, however, remove his sidearm from its holster and go through the motions of checking it to make certain it was fully loaded, whether for my benefit or for Victoria's I could not tell. Seeing the ease with which he handled the piece did reassure me, though.

Finally, after Victoria reminded me to put on my floppy hat — 'You may need it in this sun, dear' — we left.

It was still bright afternoon as we departed. Wroten looked as surprised as I felt when Victoria headed straight across the yard toward where the trail to Porcupine Falls began.

'He's at the falls?'

'Probably. Actually, it's more than a probability, considering what Effie said about him.'

I tried to think back over the few words Victoria had repeated from her friend

— 'panting like a hound dog' — but they made no sense to me. Not did Victoria offer to explain.

The trail was not difficult. It was wide enough for the three of us to walk abreast, which made talking easy although we didn't have much to say. Victoria seemed slightly preoccupied, as if she were working something out in her mind. Her eyes darted back and forth as we walked at a fairly brisk pace, slightly uphill most of the way but not too much so. She seemed capable of taking in her entire surroundings in a single glance, then her eyes would flicker in another direction. Frequently she followed something on the ground for a few dozen feet, then would look up and around. I didn't even try to figure out what she was doing.

Wroten marched along silently for the most part. I think he was half-angry, half-amused at Victoria's certainty that we would find Carver at the falls. And perhaps he was at least a bit curious — as was I — as to what was going on inside her head.

For my part, I enjoyed the hike, most of

the way through stands of pine or fir. I didn't know what species they were, but the trees were tall and thickly trunked, obviously decades if not centuries old.

'You own this land?' I asked once, entranced at the quiet, the somber beauty of the forest.

'Something over two hundred acres. It's been in my family for years. The back of the property' — she gestured in the direction we were traveling — 'abuts on national forest lands, so as long as I hold title to my acreage, I suppose one could hike for miles without ever coming across any substantial signs of civilization.'

'It must be heaven.' I remembered all too clearly, and painfully, what life had been like in Southern California.

'Yes, Lynn dear. That is exactly what it is like.'

After that, Victoria took some care to point out various types of plant life. The larger trees were mostly Jeffrey pine — she said that in the bright sunlight, the bark had a fragrance like rich caramel, and insisted that I smell one at the next opportunity. She showed me a few remnant cones from the previous winter and talked about the differences between the sizes and shapes of cones — Ponderosa (that one, Victoria sniffed, unfortunately, smelled like kerosene), Coulter, White pine.

The underbrush turned out to be as interesting as the tree cover. Stands of wild gooseberry; a small blackberry bog just off the trail, where it crossed a small stream; a narrow meadow studded with purple and white and blue and yellow flowers. I know she identified every kind of plant we passed, but to this day I don't remember most of them.

Perhaps my mind just doesn't work that way. All I saw and all I really remember were beautiful flowers and lush green stems.

Further along the trail, we passed stands of ferns. One gigantic tree had fallen ages before, so long ago that it had decayed almost to nothing and the trail passed right through what would have been the thickest part of the trunk. On either side of us, the remaining bits of wood and bark were clothed with thick moss and shelf-fungus. Some of the latter, Victoria explained, tasted wonderful when prepared properly; others were bitter or tasteless.

'Are any of them poisonous?' I asked, remembering stories about people who had gone out collecting mushrooms and ended up in emergency rooms having their stomachs pumped . . . or in morgues having entirely different kinds of operations performed on them.

'None of these, dear. There are a number of poisonous species — several quite deadly — scattered throughout these mountains. But none of these.'

Thus ended our conversations and my discoveries.

'There,' Wroten said abruptly, after we had walked for a while in silence. He pointed across the trail to a large grassy area, beyond which a stony bluff rose precipitously to a flattened ridge. Water cascaded from the bluff, sparkling over tier after tier of exposed rocks, most worn smooth from what must have been centuries of erosion.

'That's Porcupine Falls. We found the body along the edge of Redbud Creek, where it pools beneath the falls.'

He led the way as we left the hiking trail and crossed another meadow, this one larger, more lushly green than the one we had passed through earlier. The ground was mushy, not quite swampy but clearly well watered even during the driest summer months.

We hadn't progressed very far when I saw something yellow fluttering in the breeze — a vivid yellow, too uniform to be natural, crossed occasionally by black markings.

Crime scene tape.

It seemed anomalous out here, in the middle of nowhere. I'd seen samples often enough back at home. After the accident, the stretch of roadway had been completely blocked off by tape like that — 'Do not cross. Crime scene.' I had grown to hate the memory of that vivid yellow.

But up here, surrounded by trees and grass and rocks, all beneath a cloudless blue sky that seemed to go on forever . . . it seemed not only out of place but . . . obscene.

I almost couldn't approach it.

Wroten did, though, and then Victoria and I followed.

Before we were halfway there, though, I thought I saw something. Perhaps because of my distaste for the yellow tape, I had allowed my eyes to wander, away from the edge of the pool and toward the shadows along the base of the bluff itself.

'What's that?' I pointed to what looked like an oddly rounded boulder among the jumble of rocks that at some time had eroded from the cliff face onto the flat land below.

Victoria and Wroten both stopped.

Abruptly, the rounded boulder resolved itself into a hunched figure, dark with moisture from the Falls so it looked as if it were almost part of the shadows themselves.

At my words, the rock moved.

Simultaneously, Wroten shouted, 'Ellis, stop!' and Victoria, barely a breath behind him, called, rather less stridently but with a tone that nonetheless seemed to overmaster Wroten's 'Carver, you come here. Now.'

The figure froze, half standing. For another instant, it looked as if it — he — were about to leap into the pool.

Wroten strode forward a couple of paces and drew his sidearm.

'Ellis! Halt! I don't want to fire but I will!'

'Oh, for goodness' sakes!' Victoria sounded distinctly put out, although whether at Wroten for his hasty action, Carver for his stupidity in even thinking about running away, or both for their sheer man-ness in a moment of crisis, I don't know.

With a speed I would not have suspected her of possessing, certainly not at her age and not standing as we were knee-high in thick grasses and low clumps of shrubs, on soil so damp that it threatened at any moment to mire our footsteps, Victoria was suddenly between the two men, arms out, pointing one imperious hand at each of them.

'This has gone far enough. Carver, you come over here. This instant.' I noted that, however commanding her gesture might have been, she did not actually *order* Wroten to stand down. He did not holster his weapon, but he did lower it.

Carver stood for a moment longer, as if

uncertain. I was too far away to see any clear expression on his face, but in one subtle, almost unidentifiable movement, his shoulders shifted slightly, and he transformed from a man about to risk all in an effort to escape to a near-boy, disheartened, confused, and even frightened.

Wroten stalked past Victoria without speaking. I suspect that at that moment, he probably didn't trust himself to say anything to her. She didn't try to talk to him, either. Whatever she wanted to say, she had already said, in her actions as much as in her words. I moved quietly to stand next to her.

Carver stepped down a few feet from where he had been sitting and waited for Wroten to approach.

'Carver Ellis. You are under arrest for . . . for assault on an officer of the law in performance of his duty.'

I noted the hesitation. Interesting. Not as a suspect in the death of Alix Macrorie. Or perhaps just not *yet* a suspect.

Carver simply stood there until Wroten finished, then held out his hands, wrists together in the time-honored way that said, 'Okay, you got me. Where are the cuffs?'

Wroten started to pull Carver's hands behind his back to cuff him, but again Victoria intervened.

'I'm sure that won't be necessary, Deputy. We have a long way to go before we get back to your vehicle. Surely you can at least cuff him hands forward, in case he falls.'

Wroten glared his answer but reversed his movements and allowed Carver to put his wrists together in front again.

'Thank you, Deputy. And you, you foolish young man, you are going to behave yourself, aren't you.'

It was not a question, and it was almost funny in its own way. The little old lady, up to her waist in wildflowers and weeds, hands on her hips, back ramrod-straight, looking up at the young giant before her — at least he seemed a giant in comparison to her — and glaring him down.

He didn't answer beyond dropping his gaze to the ground.

'Now that that is settled,' Victoria said serenely, turning away from both Wroten and his prisoner, 'let's take a look at where you found poor Alix.'

It wasn't much. Just a stretch perhaps a dozen feet across, otherwise indistinguishable from the rest of the area. The falls were only a couple of arm lengths away, water cascading in rainbow froth into a wide pool that, as far as I could tell, extended for several hundred feet downstream. The banks were low — no doubt this meadow area flooded easily and frequently. A tumble of rocks — larger than stones, smaller than boulders — had separated farther from the rest of the bluff long before and lay scattered along the edge of the pool, evidences of the fury of past storms, no doubt. Several of the larger ones were included within the area designated by the yellow tape.

One of them, though partially damp from the pool, still showed a large, darker patch on its outer, landward edge that might have been — that probably was — crusted blood.

'She was here, half in the water. If she

fell — *if* she simply fell — she would most likely have ended up there, Doc says.' Wroten pointed to a spot a few feet away, closest to the bluff face just to the right of the falls. 'And she would probably — again *probably* — not have been caught in the water at all.

'If, on the other hand, she had gone over the falls themselves, say, from one of the larger boulders in the middle of the flow, she would most likely have been caught by the current and carried further down the stream, over that way.' Again he pointed, this time away from the falls and further downstream.

'Neither Doc nor I can quite read the scene, and he's usually pretty good at this sort of thing.'

Victoria nodded.

'Yes, I see what you mean. Half in, half out, so the force of the water could not have carried her to here. Half in, half out, so if she had been climbing along the side of the falls' — now it was her turn to point — 'over there, for instance, she would not have ended up this close to the water.'

Wroten grunted in agreement.

'Yet if she had been pushed with any force from up there,' Victoria said, pointing to the ledge immediately adjacent to the water, 'she should have drifted in the currents themselves much further. If she were murdered.'

'There might be some other possibilities,' Wroten finally said, 'after Doc determines precisely how she died. But right now, as I said earlier, we just don't know.'

I must have looked pale, because suddenly Victoria took my hand and said, 'Dear, I'm so sorry. We shouldn't have stood here talking like that. It must have been painful. Deputy Wroten, is there anything else down here we should see?'

He led the three of us — one hand firmly locked on Carver's arm — back across the meadow to the trail. From there it was only a few more minutes of fairly easy walking, back into the shadows of the trees and along a large, smoothly arcing incline until we emerged again into the sunlight.

We were now at the top of the falls, on the edge of a butte that opened into the upper valley cut eons before, when Redbud Creek was younger and wilder and more violent and more powerful.

The area closest to the creek itself, just above the falls, widened into an almost flat, hard-packed expanse, perfect for erecting a campsite.

Obviously, since this was where the troop had been heading only that morning.

Again I was startled by the realization that it was still the same day. That I had awakened only this morning to loss and anger and despair.

And then I had met Victoria Sears.

6

'You wait right here,' Wroten was saying to Carver, helping the younger man none too gently into a sitting position on the ground. 'And don't even think of getting up until I say.'

Carver still didn't respond. He had not said more than a word or two since we had found him down below the falls — perhaps his wisest decision of the day.

Victoria and Wroten headed toward a cluster of rocks that marked the top of the falls. From there they would be able to look directly down at the place where the body had first been seen. That wasn't something that I had any interest in at all.

Nor did I particularly want to stand guard over Carver. That felt distinctly awkward.

'Deputy Wroten, is there any place I shouldn't walk?'

He turned to face me.

'There have been so many pairs of feet

straying over this area already today that one more probably won't make any difference. I've marked a few places that will need to be examined more closely' — he pointed to a small tag positioned on a rough circle of rocks. From the evidences of smoke on the inside, that would be the fire pit where Alix and . . . whoever . . . prepared . . . whatever had been in the mess-kit. 'Don't disturb any of those.'

I nodded my agreement and headed directly away from the fire pit, toward the closest bank of the creek, some yards above where the water emptied over the falls.

The camping area itself seemed dry, almost gravely in places, roughly a square about twenty-five to thirty yards across. I'm a poor judge of distances, but there seemed to be enough space for a few tents and corresponding fire-rings, with enough room left over for rough-housing and other appropriate boy-type activities. I could easily imagine why the troop enjoyed coming here.

Carver was roughly in the middle of the

plot, sitting cross-legged in the dirt, his hands — securely cuffed — dangling listlessly over his knees. His shoulders were slumped and his head bowed.

From my perspective, I had never seen a less likely suspect for murder, or for flight from the law.

I wandered along the edge of the creek for a few dozen feet, crossed into the meadow, trying to avoid crushing more plants than necessary, then sat on the top of a largish boulder that jutted up from among the greenery.

From there, I could see the length of the creek on one hand, rippling in the afternoon sun until it disappeared around a distant bend. On the other, Victoria and Wroten stood, outlined against blue sky, as if they were perched on the edge of the world.

Straight ahead, the meadow filled the area between water and tree line. I couldn't remember ever having seen such startling, vital green, studded throughout with white and cream and yellow flowers, with hints here and there of scarlet and purple.

When my mind began turning toward what had brought us here — to images of broken bodies bleeding on rocks, or other bodies, equally shattered and torn in the wreckage of a car — I forced myself to think of something else. Anything else.

What had Victoria said earlier that morning as she had given me a tour of her garden, pointing out this wildflower or the other? How many names of them could I remember? How many were growing wild in this meadow?

We had passed a small patch of yarrow just before we reached the camping site. I remembered the umbrella-like heads, what seemed like hundreds of tiny white flowers clustered in a circle around the stem, the grey-green leaves so finely divided that they seemed like feathers. What had she called it: yes, *Achillea millifolium*. Named for Achilles, who supposedly used the plant as a medicine for his troops; and for the thousand-seeming leaves that could be stewed to make a tea, a preventative against colds. Victoria had pinched off a tiny bit of leaf from her garden and given it to me to try

— bitter and pungent, astringent, but with an undertaste that might actually have been pleasant . . . with sufficient sweetening.

What else was there?

I climbed down from the boulder and began moving slowly through the growth.

There were tiny yellow flowers at my feet, low, creeping on deep green leaves. Buttercups. *Cinquefoil* — five-petals. And not too much farther away, a vivid splash of purple, petals folded back almost against the stem. That was a Shooting Star — easy enough to recall.

A bit of dark blue rising a couple of feet above the ground. That was the larkspur. It reminded me of the delphiniums that my mother had grown in our front yard when I was a child. Victoria had told me that the plant was poisonous, filled with alkeloids that would lead to vomiting and, unless purged, death.

Death . . . amid all of this beauty.

Further off, there was even more death.

I could see a small stand of large plants, bright yellow-green, with enormous veined leaves that folded around the stalks at the base. They were perhaps five feet tall, growing in a small depression where, I assumed, water would pool whenever it rained. Perhaps there was a small rivulet from the creek that kept the ground wet throughout the summer.

At any rate, I recognized what Victoria had called Corn Lily. False Hellebore. True Hellebore, she had explained, at least had had some medicinal properties for ancient cultures. False Hellebore, however, *Devil's Bite*, was simply toxic. She had recounted a grimly fascinating anecdote about it. Centuries before, native tribes would elect their leaders by having all of the candidates gather around and eat a small bit of False Hellebore. The last one to vomit won.

I suppose that if any of them had been stubborn enough to resist the urge, they would have died — thus eliminating at least a portion of the stubborn and stupid genes from the community.

Either way, death again.

I looked the other way, back toward where Victoria and Wroten were still talking, where Carver was still sitting motionless in the dirt, and decided that I had had enough. I began making my way back to them.

Just before I broke through the vegetation to the drier areas, I passed one more plant that I recognized.

This one was tall, as tall as the False Hellebore, but with long, narrow, jaggedly edged leaves, and large, lacy umbrellas of white flowers — very like yarrow but without the feathery effect.

Queen Anne's Lace.

I stopped to examine it more closely. The flower-heads really did resemble the crochet pattern Victoria had shown me earlier. They were beautiful, delicate, like fragile open-work. And at least this plant was not deadly. It was called wild carrot, in fact, because — as Victoria had explained it — the roots smelled very like garden-variety carrots. And the plant was edible: flowers, leaves, roots. Everything.

Its rather horrific common name — *Devil's Plague* — came from the fact that, because it produced seeds in such prolific amounts, once the plant took root in an area, it was almost impossible to get rid of.

But at least, it was not a bringer of death.

I straightened, but before I could take a step toward the others at the head of the falls, something caught my eye.

A glint. Something metallic.

Stooping, I found that I had nearly trodden on a pocket knife. The blades were retracted and the handle was muddy, but enough metal showed through to catch the sunlight and draw my attention.

Perhaps it was something important.

I debated leaving the knife where it was but was not certain I would find it again, so I knelt down on the damp earth — staining my jeans along the way, I later discovered — and picked it up using the tail of my blouse.

Perhaps I had found a clue.

Victoria and Wroten had apparently finished talking over whatever it was that had interested them at the top of the falls. They had returned to the camping area and Wroten was helping Carver struggle to his feet. It looked as if, having sat in one position for so long, he was having difficulty getting his legs to support his weight, because Wroten was basically hauling the younger man up. Victoria was hovering nearby — if someone as inherently dignified as Victoria could be said to *hover* — as if preparing to catch Carver should he collapse.

By the time I got close enough to talk to them, Carver seemed upright and stable, although still distinctly sullen and dejected.

'I found something over there,' I said. 'It might be helpful.'

I handed the knife to Wroten, careful to keep from touching it with my fingers. He used his handkerchief to receive it.

The knife was closed. It was about five inches long, with an inlay of some kind of dark, richly grained wood along the body.

Wroten studied it for a few moments, then carefully opened the longer of the two blades.

'Good knife,' he said finally. 'It's a Queen.'

I must have looked blank, because he glanced at me before explaining further.

'Queen's a brand-name. It's one of the

better makes, or at least one of the more expensive. This wood is called birdseye maple, because of the grain. It's fairly rare. Knife like this would probably run a hundred and twenty dollars. Not something anyone would be likely to just drop and leave.'

He turned to Carver.

'Ever see it before?'

Carver shook his head.

Victoria extended her hand and Wroten placed it in her palm.

'I've never seen it before, either,' she said after a brief inspection. 'But I see what you mean about it being expensive.'

She indicated one side of the blade. It was beautifully engraved with a bird in the center and initials on either side. The whole figure was surrounded with fine filigree lines that swirled and coiled about each other.

'An eagle,' Victoria went on. 'With wings spread — I think the term in heraldry is 'displayed' — and an ornate 'B' and 'D.'' She hesitated for a moment before turning to Carver. 'Do you know anyone with those initials?'

He shook his head again.

'Hmmm.'

'Do they mean anything to you, Miz Sears?' Wroten retrieved the knife, closed it, and put it in a plastic bag before slipping it into his pocket.

'I'm not sure. I'll have to think about it.'

He waited for her to continue, but instead of speaking, she re-traced my steps through the meadow toward the spot where I had found the knife.

I started to follow, but Wroten put his hand on my arm to stop me.

'She's looking for something.'

He was apparently correct. Victoria studied the area closely for a few moments, then bent over to inspect something. She didn't kneel — she was smarter about that than I had been — and she didn't touch anything . . . just looked, then straightened, and returned.

'Anything?' Wroten asked.

She didn't answer directly. Instead she glanced at the sky and said, 'If we don't start back now, it will be dark before we get to my place.'

Without waiting for a response, she began walking toward where the trail disappeared into the trees. Wroten and Carver followed. I brought up the rear.

We spoke very little on the return hike. Victoria seemed caught up in her own thoughts. Occasionally she would murmur something, as if working out an idea, but she made no offer to share. Once or twice Wroten started to ask her something but when she pointedly ignored him, he finally quit. Carver marched stolidly along, neither speaking nor answering.

I followed in silence.

The trail was much darker than it had been earlier in the day.

Deeper in shadow, cooler. Several times along the way, I found myself almost shivering, although whether because of the cold or because of what had happened back there — the violence, the death, overshadowing the natural peacefulness of the place — I was not sure.

Wroten kept Carver by his side, occasionally assisting the younger man over rough patches in the trail, keeping him from stumbling and falling. He didn't remove the cuffs, however, and there was no mistaking the fact that he clearly considered Carver his prisoner.

Victoria and I followed. She kept a hand on my arm as well, but not to support me. There was hardly any weight to her touch at all. Instead, she seemed to be merely reminding me that there was someone else there with me, someone who understood my reactions to the scene of dying and death. She said almost nothing to me, and I didn't feel that it was up to me to break the stillness.

The four of us followed the trail downhill without incident. It seemed to take far less time than the earlier trek.

When we arrived at Victoria's house, Wroten steered Carver directly toward the patrol car.

'You're not taking him in, are you, Deputy Wroten,' Victoria protested. 'I'm sure he had nothing to do with Alix's death.'

Carver seemed to wither at the sound of the girl's name.

Wroten shook his head. 'I don't know about that, Miz Sears. Maybe. Maybe not. Not directly, at least. But he's involved in some way, and until I find out how, he's going with me. Anyway, he did assault an officer of the law investigating the death. That tells me that he's at least a person of interest. I'm going to keep him overnight. Tomorrow, Doc will give me his report, and perhaps we can clear this up then.'

Victoria removed her hand from my arm and placed it reassuringly on Carver's.

'Don't worry. I know you couldn't harm Alix. We'll settle all of this tomorrow. Just be patient.'

For a change, Carver nodded rather than shook his head. 'Thanks, Miz Sears.'

She watched as Wroten and his prisoner got into the car, backed down the drive, and disappeared.

'I guess I had better get going,' I said. 'It's getting on toward dark.'

'Nonsense. You're not going anywhere tonight, Lynn dear. You're going to come inside, have supper here, and spend the night in my guest room.'

I started to protest but Victoria cut me off with a wave of her hand.

'It gets lonely out here sometimes, especially at night. It will be delightful to have someone to chat with, and besides, I have to check on your wrist.'

I was startled. Throughout the entire afternoon, including two long hikes and my private wandering through the meadow at the falls, I had nearly forgotten the sling on my arm and the bandage on my wrist.

I took quick stock. The wrist hurt a little, a distant throb that seemed merely the echo of the earlier pain. Certainly not a break. Probably not even a serious sprain.

'Really, I think it is all right,' I said. 'And I don't want to impose on you any more . . . '

'It's no imposition, dear. It's a pleasure.'

It didn't strike me at the time that Victoria knew about today's importance to me. She had mentioned Terry and Shawn only in passing when we had first met, and — to be honest — I had forgotten that she knew. Indeed, for large portions of the day, even *I* had forgotten.

A year ago today.

Only later did I realize the obvious fact

that Victoria simply didn't want me to be alone that night, alone with my memories and the shadows of the past. Death had been too much on our minds that day.

By that time, she had gently but firmly guided me through the living room and into the kitchen. She switched on the lights. I hadn't realized how advanced the twilight had been until then.

The kitchen was large, brightly painted, with everything polished and in its place.

Again I tried to remonstrate with her, but she was already bustling around, pulling this and that from the refrigerator or the pantry shelves, indicating with a quick flick of her wrist the plates to be set on the table, which drawer the silverware was in, which glasses to use.

Almost before I had the table ready, she was putting fresh salad, slices of cold ham, more thick hunks of homemade bread, and a small bowl of tomatoes between the plates.

'It will just be catch-as-catch-can, tonight. I told you that it wouldn't be any imposition. This is what I would have prepared for myself, and your being here is just an added blessing.'

We ate quietly, chatting companionably about inconsequentialities. I learned a little about Victoria's life — her marriage half a century earlier, her husband's untimely death from cancer before they had an opportunity to raise a family, her settling on the family acres, and her contentment with the life she had led since then. She learned a bit more about me, including some memories of childhood vacations spent in mountains — no where near Fox Creek, of course, but in landscapes similar enough for us to share a few stories.

After we cleaned up, she invited me to relax in the living room while she made a few telephone calls.

'Just a few things that came to mind today while we were out. Perhaps I can help Detective Wroten tomorrow if I check around a little myself. Purely unofficially, of course. I wouldn't want to step on anyone's toes.'

I hadn't realized quite how tired I was, in spite of knowing intellectually how much of a toll the day must have taken.

Sitting in Victoria's hushed living room, hearing the sound of an old-fashioned clock ticking on the mantle, the low buzzing of her voice as she talked on the telephone, the faint sounds of nighttime settling down over the forest . . . without becoming aware of any change, I drifted into a gentle, dreamless sleep.

By the same clock, it was an hour or so later when she roused me.

'Oh, I'm so sorry, Victoria. I didn't mean to . . . '

'Never mind about that. I could tell that you were getting tired. You deserved a chance to rest.'

'I didn't intend to be an inconsiderate guest, drifting off like that.' She chuckled.

'It has something to do with the mountain air,' she said finally. 'It can be unnervingly relaxing at times, especially after a stressful day.'

We talked a bit longer, again nothing of any importance. Neither of us felt that we wanted to bring up our thoughts about Alix, or Carver and Prescott, or what we had seen at the falls. For the moment, we were content to let others — Wroten chief among them — shoulder that burden.

Finally, it was time for bed. Victoria lent me a long flannel nightgown and showed me around the guest bedroom and bath. The bed was still slightly wrinkled from where young Toby had napped earlier that morning, and a lightweight crocheted throw lay rumpled at the foot.

She straightened the bed covers, turning them down with a professional ease, folding the throw neatly into a square and sliding it onto a shelf in the closet.

Satisfied, she wished me good night and gently closed the door as she left.

Surprisingly, in light of my nap not too long before, I fell right asleep.

It must have been about 4:00 the next morning when I woke to a faint tap on my shoulder and Victoria's voice saying in my ear, 'Lynn dear, I need you to wake up.'

Given the events of the past day, I was not surprised to find myself sitting upright and fully awake even before she had finished her sentence.

Upright and awake, perhaps, but it still

took me several moments to adjust to what I was seeing and realize that I was in an unfamiliar bed, in an unfamiliar room. I must have stared around questioningly, because Victoria's voice came again . . . although this time without the accompanying tap.

'Lynn, I need you to wake up.'

'I'm awake, Victoria. What is it?'

I started to throw the covers back, half in a panic all of a sudden, but she laid her hand on my shoulder and said, 'It's nothing to worry about, dear. There's no need for alarm. Take a deep breath.'

I did, then repeated my question. 'What is it?'

'Someone has just gone up the trail to the falls.'

Again I must have looked slightly quizzical.

'Porcupine Falls. Where Alix . . . '

'Yes.'

'Someone just went past the house and turned up the trail. I am going to follow. Would you be willing to come with me?'

'But what if . . . don't you think that it might be . . . '

'I'm quite sure that there is no danger. But I think we might learn a few important things about Alix's death if we follow. Will you come?'

I stepped out of the bed. 'Certainly. Give me a few minutes to dress.'

She stepped back. I noticed that she was fully clothed in outside gear — hiking boots, jeans, a flannel shirt, and a light jacket.

'You'll find sweaters and a couple of jackets in that closet. Find one that fits. It's liable to be cool outside, particularly in the moist air by the falls.'

I nodded and she left the room. I slipped out of the nightgown — abruptly aware of how warm and comforting it had been — and pulled on my own clothing. They felt stiff and slightly damp.

In a few more moments, I was dressed warmly, thanks to a denim jacket with a thin woolly lining that felt just as warm and as comforting as the nightgown had.

I went into the kitchen.

Victoria had only a single light on, so the room was still rather dark, shadowy. She was standing by the rear door holding a couple of small flashlights — penlights, really, I discovered when I took the one she held out to me.

'They should give us enough light. It's quite bright out, with no clouds. And the trail isn't rough at all. I know it well enough to hike it without a light, but better safe . . . '

She turned to leave. She was wearing a strange device over her shoulder. It hung against her back rather like an empty arrow quiver, several inches across and perhaps fifteen inches or so long. It seemed to be made of metal.

'What's that . . . ?' I started to ask, but she motioned me to silence with one hand.

'We must be as quiet as possible. I think he . . . whoever it is . . . is far enough ahead not to hear us, but sound travels easily up here at night. We don't want to spook him.'

'Do you know who . . . ?'

But again she motioned me to silence.

7

By that time we were outside. She shut the door carefully, making practically no noise, and while neither of us quite went tip-toe, we both took some pains to avoid unnecessary sounds. Our footsteps *crunch-crunch-crunch*-ed along a short patch of gravel behind the house, then became the merest whisper of *thumps* as we passed on to the well-packed trail itself.

Victoria walked beside me, her hand again resting lightly on my arm. She indicated with her own flash that we should aim the lights toward our feet, showing as little as possible to anyone who might be ahead on the trail and happen to look back.

She was correct. The trail was smooth enough, but even the faint illumination of the penlights, aimed as they were at the ground, was sufficient to transform everything around me into deep shadow. I don't know if Victoria could see very far ahead . . . she never faltered in her steps. But for me, it was as if I were walking through blackness so complete as to be almost tangible, except for the small round spots that highlighted our feet.

We walked in silence.

She had also been right about the night air. It was cool — cool enough that the light jackets were wonderfully warming. They, along with the heat we generated by our exertions, made the night seem pleasant. The air was still slightly tinted with the smells of daytime — hints of pine and fir, the dampness of moss on the rocks as we passed by small ponds, the soil itself, rich with the humus of centuries of decayed plants . . . and, of course, animals.

As I became acclimated to the stillness that surrounded us, I began hearing small noises, nothing particularly threatening in itself but discomforting to a city dweller like myself. At first it was only small cracks and thumps in the darkness. The first time I heard something, I must have jumped slightly, because Victoria's grip on my arm tightened momentarily and she whispered, so softly that it sounded as if her lips were right up against my ear, 'It's just a pine cone falling. Nothing to worry about.'

Gradually, though, it seemed as if I could hear faint movement in the undergrowth that edged the trail, furtive skittering and rustling that might have been small animals — squirrels or chipmunks, perhaps. I hoped — because the only other small animals I could think of at the moment were rats (a further legacy of my usual habitat), and I didn't even want to think of anything quick and furry scuttering across my feet.

Once in a while, something larger clattered through the trees, distantly and feebly, as if far enough from us that whatever it had been was neither afraid of us nor threatening to us.

'A deer, probably,' Victoria whispered, once again grasping my arm reassuringly.

Perhaps fifteen or twenty minutes into our journey, I happened to slip slightly, nearly losing my footing, and before Victoria could stabilize me, I had flicked the light upward and to the side. It glimmered off the smooth, glossy surface of some shrubs that stood nearly waist high to me, and then beyond, in the depths of the darkness, it caught and reflected two great eyes, round and unblinking and glassy against the featureless background.

I caught my breath and might even have made a small hiss of surprise. The eyes remained for another instant, then disappeared as abruptly as they had appeared — at one moment there, gleaming and deep with mystery and suggestions of the unknown, the next moment vanished as silently and completely as if they had never been.

Victoria didn't say anything. Perhaps she hadn't noticed the eyes in the moment of helping me correct my slip and keep from falling. At any rate, we walked a few paces further on as I imagined what might have been there: deer, perhaps; or possibly a fox, since the eyes reminded me of having occasionally caught a dog's glare in my headlights as I angled up my driveway at night; or perhaps a raccoon, even a small mountain cat of some sort, although I was under the impression that cats, while present in the area, were timid and avoided humans where possible.

The whole effect of the hike was becoming increasingly eerie, ethereal, otherworldly, with sounds and sights that, while I might have easily recognized them by day, came at me from new perspectives.

Tree trunks slid past, barely discernible in the faint light, moving as if of their own volition, as silently as our own footsteps. The bark might catch an errant gleam and, for a moment, seem gilded or silvered over the black backdrop, then the moment would pass and abruptly the shape would fade into nothingness.

Like people in my life, I thought at one point. Like Terry and Shawn — there one minute, and then within the expanse of a blink, gone forever, almost before I could truly know them or understand them.

Like Alix, whom I never knew in person but who had become for me as real, as individual and unique, and as fleeting as the trees beside me.

For a moment, I felt tears welling up. Then I blinked my eyes and sternly reminded myself why I was out there, that someone had passed this way, perhaps only minutes before, someone who might hold a key to understanding Alix's death.

At least, that is what Victoria had intimated.

And what I hoped.

Finally, after an interminable-seeming time, in which nothing felt familiar, in which I could recognize none of the land-marks that had dotted that trail during my two trips along it in the daytime, Victoria grasped my arm and pulled me gently back.

'One more ridge,' she whispered. 'The campground . . . just up there.'

We moved on, more slowly and more carefully, trying to make even less noise in our passage, keeping to one side of the trail where the bulk of the trees might hide us from anyone at the top of the Falls.

After a few more steps, Victoria flicked off her penlight. I did the same. The night instantly encompassed us, but after only a short while, shapes and shadows began forming themselves out of the blackness.

Stars glimmered overhead . . . and just beyond, what looked like only a dozen yards or so from where we stood, a thin light moved back and forth across the surface of the camping area.

Victoria indicated with a movement of her arm that we should creep forward. A few more steps, as we could see, clearly silhouetted against a distant sky, a single figure, bent as if searching. As it moved, the light moved as well, sweeping slowly along the rocks and low shrubbery that studded the edge of the camping sites.

Back and forth, back and forth — the light swung evenly yet cautiously, as if the figure were examining every inch of the ground, meticulously, looking for something specific, something that must have been important to him . . . or her.

Abruptly Victoria straightened and lifted her arm from mine. She took another few steps forward, approaching the figure and the light. I remained where I was, barely daring to breathe.

Then, just as abruptly, Victoria switched her small light on. The penlight streamed like a searchlight across the open space, falling squarely on the back of the figure. It must have seen an alteration in the light and shadow before it, because it turned slowly and raised its own flash.

'I don't think you will find anything there, Lance,' Victoria said quietly, gently, as if being careful not to startle the other person . . . Lance Prescott. 'It's a wasted effort, I'm afraid.'

'Who . . . Victoria?' He sounded simultaneously terrified, incredulous, cautious, and startled. 'What . . . ?'

'I heard you pass my house earlier. You could only have been coming up here.'

'I tried . . . I *know* I didn't make any noise when I went by. I *know* I didn't.'

'Even so, I heard you. And Lynn and I came up here to bring you back down.'

'Lynn . . . Mrs. Hanson?' He raised his flashlight to pinion me where I was waiting some paces behind Victoria.

I shuddered. What if he were the murderer? What if he was afraid we would find out? What if he . . . ?

Suddenly he pivoted on one foot and began running. He hadn't gone more than a dozen feet when two things happened.

First, Victoria raised her voice for the first time that night. 'Get back here, you young fool!'

And second, he must have tripped over a low rock because abruptly the shadowy figure disappeared and a harsh yelp rose from the other side of the campground.

'I can't believe this,' Victoria muttered under her breath as she hurried across to where Prescott had fallen. I ran behind her, my penlight jiggling up and down with each step, casting eerie shadows all around.

By the time I arrived, Victoria had helped Prescott to his feet. He was bent over, brushing at the knees of his pants.

' . . . ridiculous stunt,' Victoria was saying. 'And for no reason.'

'Look, Victoria, I didn't . . . '

'Right now, I don't want to hear what you did do or did not do. That will all sort itself out. Right now I want to hear from you that you will stand right here with Lynn and not move a muscle until I return.'

'Where . . . ?' Prescott and I began our questions in almost the same breath. Victoria merely shook her head at us.

'I want both of you to stay here. Lance, you behave yourself. And Lynn, you . . . well, you can keep this young idiot company for a few minutes.'

With that she disappeared out of the small ring of light that surrounded us. We followed the glow of her light for a short while, but then she apparently moved from the flat camping area into the meadow just beyond, where there was enough brush and low shrubs to obscure her completely.

We stood there, silently, neither of us willing to break the stillness around us. Off in the distance, I thought I heard a rustling of leaves, as if Victoria were moving through a stand of some kind of plants, but I couldn't be sure. I could hear Prescott's breathing, harsh and ragged, not so much from the exertion of his short run, I was sure, as from whatever emotion was raging inside him. I wanted to ask him what Victoria knew, what he had been searching for, how it all tied in to Alix Macrorie's death — because I was certain that it did tie in.

But because neither of us knew the

other well enough to encroach on the noiselessness of the night, because neither of us knew the other well enough to trust unspoken motives and understandings — I might, after all, be standing next to a murderer — we chose not to break that silence.

I suppose Victoria was only gone five minutes or so. It seemed much longer than that. But finally we heard a distinct rustling coming from the direction she had disappeared into, and a moment later her form solidified from the shadows.

'All right, then. Are we ready?'

Prescott apparently felt the need to make one more try.

'You've got to believe me . . . '

'What I've got to believe is that you are coming back down with Lynn and me. That you will wait at my place until Deputy Wroten can bring Doc Anderson and Ellis Carver up from town. And that you will tell us the truth — the whole and exact truth — along with everyone else involved, so that we can settle this matter once and for all. Clear?'

He nodded. Victoria started toward the

trail. Prescott followed, but almost immediately halted with a groan.

'My ankle.'

Rather to my amazement, Victoria retraced her steps, knelt down in the shadows, and felt along the contours of his foot. She apparently pressed here and there, because he would mumble a 'Yes' or 'No' to her repeated 'Does this hurt?'

Finally she must have been satisfied.

'Nothing broken. Probably not even sprained. Most likely twisted. We'll take it easy on the way down, though.'

She turned to face the man directly. It was rather comical, since he towered over her by a good head but it seemed to all the world as if she was totally in charge. And in fact, she was.

'Now, Lynn and I probably couldn't do much to stop you if you decided to head out for parts unknown. But you probably wouldn't get far afoot, especially if you've strained your ankle, before Deputy Wroten, the State Police, the Forest Service, and everyone else this side of the Rockies with a badge and a gun tracked you down. And someone is very likely to get hurt if that happens.

'And that someone is *you*.

'So I strongly recommend you turn yourself around and come with us.'

Prescott stood for a moment, his shoulders squared as if in defiance — or at least as if he were contemplating defiance — then he slumped slightly and dropped his hands until his light was pointing at his feet.

'Right,' Victoria said simply. There was no sense of triumph or gloating in her voice, nothing that sounded like other than her usual every-day conversational tone. 'Then let's get going. I want to get home before daylight.'

She began moving again toward the trail. She did not look back to assure herself that we were following. She simply took that as a given.

As she turned, I noticed that the odd quiver-like apparatus she had put on at the house looked different. With the pale light and the shifting shadows of Prescott's body intervening between us, it took me a few moments to realize that she had placed something in the tube.

After a few more minutes, I finally decided that whatever it was, she had wrapped in newspaper, which stuck six inches or so above the tube in a kind of florist's cone. Beyond that, I could see only shadows.

We began walking.

It's one of the mysteries of travel that the journey outward almost always seems much longer than the journey back. The night-time hike up the trail had felt as if it had taken hours — the darkness, the shadows, the silence, the tiny circles of light that outlined our feet and the next step or two that we would take.

Returning along the same trail seemed a matter of minutes rather than hours. We did not need to keep silent, although there was precious little talking among us. But at least we could shine our light straight ahead rather than at our feet, and since Prescott had brought a much stronger flash than our little penlights — a four-cell emergency light, in fact — the trail was well illuminated. There were none of the mysterious ebbing and flowing of shadows, none of the moments of half-fear when it seemed as if something just beyond my vision were about to flow over me and engulf me.

Victoria went first, with the strongest flashlight. Her steps were firm and regular. She knew the trail, and even by night it held no surprises.

Prescott followed. He limped slightly at first, but after a while even that disappeared and he shuffled along behind Victoria, neither speaking or making any effort to move ahead or fall behind.

I brought up the rear. It was not a particularly irksome task. Victoria set a mild enough pace for me, and by following her and Prescott, I had no difficulty keeping my footing.

Perhaps because there was more light, perhaps because there were more people — by one, at any rate — with me, but now I seemed to hear fewer errant sounds, fewer rustles and creaks and thumps. There was really nothing except the fall of boots against hard-packed soil, and the light swish of fabric against fabric as arms swung back and forth and legs rose and fell.

By the time Victoria's house hove into view, a thin blade of light was breaking over the distant ridges. Darkness had been replaced by faint shadows that gradually but inexorably became more sharply delineated. The sky began taking on a rosy tint, and the tops of the trees around us could be seen clearly against the light. The long night was over.

8

'Straight into the kitchen,' Victoria directed as soon as we were inside and had taken off our jackets. 'You two have a seat at the table. I'm going to call Deputy Wroten, and then I'm going to fix us all something to eat.'

That sounded good to me. After all of the hiking during the previous hours, I was famished. I glanced over at Prescott.

He looked horrible. Part of it might have been hunger — I knew from what Victoria had said about him that he had been 'living off the land' and I didn't know how competent he might be at that. And he had to have been up at least a couple of hours longer than we had, to hike down from the line cabin, past Victoria's place, and on up to the falls. In fact, he looked as if he hadn't slept at all last night . . . perhaps not the night before, either. He was pale if not ashen, and I could tell that that wasn't his normal coloration. He had been spending a goodly amount of time outdoors; he probably sported a healthy tan under more natural circumstances. He was disheveled as well, not only in his clothing — which clearly were the same he had been wearing yesterday — but in his general appearance . . . unshaven, his hair unruly and wild. His eyes seemed hollowed, red-circled, and downcast.

He showed every sign of guilt . . . of something.

I just didn't know what.

By the time we were seated and comfortable — as comfortable as we were going to be — around the large oak table, Victoria had nearly finished her telephone call.

'All right, then. All of you. In about an hour. That would be fine. Thank you. Goodbye.'

She turned to us.

'Deputy Wroten has agreed to conduct his investigation here, closer to where things took place. That makes it easier. He will be here shortly, along with Doc Anderson and Ellis Carver.'

She cast a meaningful glance at Prescott.

'And I expect you to behave yourself this time, Lance. No more of that foolishness from yesterday. It's high time we got everything sorted out. Finally.'

Prescott didn't speak. He sat with his head down, as if counting the individual grains in the oak planks in front of him.

Victoria moved over to the counter and began taking out cooking ingredients.

'How can I help?' I started to rise but she indicated by a gesture that I should remain seated.

'I've cooked alone in this kitchen for so many years now that I wouldn't know what to do with another person scurrying around with me. You must be exhausted. Just rest there.'

She pulled out a few more things, then called over her shoulder, 'Lance, would you prefer fresh-cut elderflower fritters or regular pancakes? There's a bush at the corner of the house that is just about ready. It won't take me a moment to cut some'

She turned full around and spoke to me before Lance could answer.

'It's one of the secrets of the outdoors up here. Clip the large elderberry clusters and dip the heads — actually hundreds of tiny white flowers — in a light pancake batter and fry them. Tastes delicious.'

Lance made a slight noise. I looked over at him. As pale as he had been when we sat down, he was even whiter now, as if every ounce of color had drained from his cheeks. His face worked as if he were trying to say something, but finally he just shook his head mutely.

'All right, regular pancakes it is,' Victoria said sweetly. She seemed oddly pleased, curiously pleased with something. Perhaps she merely hadn't relished going back outside to harvest the flowers.

It only took her a few minutes of measuring and pouring and whipping and stirring and cooking before she presented us with a plateful of what turned out to be the most luscious pancakes I had ever eaten — light, crisp along the edges, done just to perfection through the center.

She placed several jars on the table as well.

'Honey,' she said, pointing to one.

'Raspberry jelly. And chokecherry syrup. Made it myself last fall.'

I chose the jelly. Prescott seemed satisfied with a pat of butter — nothing else.

'Chokecherries,' she continued, 'grow wild further up the mountains. They're highly astringent when they are red and nearing ripening, only less so when they turn black and are fully ripe. It takes gallons of sugar, it seems, to tame the bitterness, but then the syrup can't be beat.'

She poured a generous helping on her own pancakes.

'The curious thing about them is that most folks wouldn't be caught dead — if you'll excuse my saying so — eating anything that has the word 'choke' in the name. They are so bitter when eaten right off the tree that it seems like they must be poisonous, and a goodly number of people firmly believe that they are.

'Bear and raccoons know differently, and will often strip the plants of any ripe berries before we humans even get a chance to pick any.

'Of course, once the leaves start to wilt, the plant *is* toxic for horses that graze on it. The leaves release prussic acid, a form of cyanide, that doesn't set well with horses. A few pounds of the leaves as forage can kill stock.'

Finally, she persuaded me to try a bit. And she was right. It was delicious.

'I'll give you a couple of bottles to take home with you,' she said as she rose to clear the table.

I noticed that Prescott had eaten very little. His plate was still nearly full.

'Settle yourselves in the living room,' Victoria said. 'It will only take me a couple of minutes to clean this up, then we can all sit and rest.'

As I had the day before, I offered to lend a hand. But this time, for whatever reason, she was adamant. I was to relax and wait with Prescott in the other room. She would take care of all the cleaning up that was necessary.

Prescott and I made our way into the front room and sat down . . . each in the chair that we had occupied the previous afternoon. We stared uncomfortably at each other for a moment, then tried to find something interesting to pin our attention on — a picture, a hand-turned lamp, a window dressing. Neither of us were particularly successful.

After a while, Victoria entered. She carried a cut-glass vase with a few flowers, crossed the room, and positioned the vase neatly on the end of the mantle. From my seat, I could recognize the white dome-shaped clusters of Queen Anne's Lace and a few of the raggedly cut leaves.

They were attractive enough, but it seemed unusual for Victoria to be taking the time to decorate the living room. Wroten and the others would be arriving any time now, and then we would be involved in far more serious things — death and murder.

Victoria sat in her usual seat and picked up her knitting and began clicking away with the needles, apparently starting where she had been interrupted the previous afternoon.

I found it almost impossible to tear my eyes away from the intricate, incessant movement of the needles, flashing in the soft light, moving back and forth in what seemed like pre-ordained patterns. It was hypnotic, in its own way.

Abruptly, she laid the needles aside, removed her knitting things from her lap, and stood.

'The others are here.'

I hadn't heard anything, but the moment she spoke I became aware of a car crunching up the driveway. We waited, unmoving, until the car came to a halt, the doors opened and slammed shut, and several figures approached the porch.

Victoria went to the door to welcome them.

Deputy Wroten came in first, then Ellis Carver, hands behind his back and cuffed. The older man was Doc Anderson — I had gotten only a glimpse of him the day before as the body had been loaded into the coroner's van. Roy Mintern followed, looking uncertain and disconcerted. I wondered why he was there, then remembered that he had found the body. Bringing up the rear was another deputy.

Wroten introduced the other officer. 'Ewart Allen, my second in command.'

Allen nodded to each of us in turn, touched the brim of his hat briefly when he faced Victoria, then removed it.

She indicated that the men were to be seated. It seemed odd at the time, but she appeared to be more in charge than Wroten.

'And for heaven's sake, Deputy, take those silly things off Carver. There's no need to over-react. He's not going anywhere. Not today.' She glared at Carver, who dropped his eyes to stare at the floor.

'No one is going anywhere. Not until we unscramble this mess.'

Wroten looked as if he were about to object, then clearly changed his mind and unlocked the cuffs, slipping them back onto his belt. Carver rubbed his wrists — perhaps a bit theatrically — then dropped into the nearest chair.

Doc Anderson crossed the room and knelt beside me.

'Miz Sears says you hurt your arm yesterday . . . '

'That can wait, can't it, Doc?' Wroten interrupted. 'We're here to . . . '

'The dead are dead,' Doc said,

147

unwrapping my wrist and gently feeling along the bone and muscles. 'We can do nothing for them. Let them rest. Let me tend to the living first.'

He checked on the progress of my sprained wrist — far less painful than yesterday and barely swollen any more — with Lance sitting quietly, watching as closely as if he were the one under the knife. There was something odd in his gaze, but I couldn't figure it out.

No one said anything more until Doc had finished his examination and re-wrapped my wrist.

'Victoria was right. A bad strain. Just remember though, move slowly, get as much rest as you can. You'll probably feel pretty stiff for a while. But everything should be all right in a few days.'

He stood and settled into a chair along the wall.

We all looked toward Wroten, expecting him to begin his interrogations, but the first voice that spoke took me by surprise.

'Well,' Victoria said. Her voice was soft, but it carried through the room. And then she said the oddest thing: 'I suppose you're wondering why I called you here.'

She smiled, an impish, mischievous smile that dropped twenty years from her face and made it impossible to believe that she was an old woman.

'Sorry, Deputy Wroten,' she said, turning her attention to him and smiling — just a hint of a smile — 'but I just had to say that. I've read too many mystery novels not to know how the detective is supposed to act.'

Then the smile faded and she dropped her eyes. 'I'm sorry. I shouldn't have said that. This is not a novel, and it is not a time for inappropriate humor, either.' She looked up 'The fact is, we have a death to unravel.'

Wroten stared at her for a moment before speaking. When he began, it was as if he had chosen to ignore her interruption.

'Things have changed since yesterday. Become a bit clearer, in some ways, but also more complicated. I'm going to let Doc begin.'

He didn't sit down but moved toward the side, turning the floor over to Doc but retaining his position of authority.

'Yes. Well. To begin with, Alix Macrorie did not drown.'

Several heads nodded. The body had apparently been too battered, too broken.

'Nor did she die as a consequence of falling.'

So . . . it *was* murder.

'Nor, in fact, were any of her injuries the cause of her death. They all occurred post-mortem.'

Doc was a born actor. Each of his pronouncements was followed by a pause, dramatic in effect, as if framed to elicit the strongest response from his listeners. And it was working. Every eye was on him, even Wroten's, although the Deputy surely already knew what Doc was about to say.

'Alix Macrorie was poisoned.'

A murmur spread through the room. Eyes shifted back and forth, taking in every expression. Only Victoria seemed unfazed by Doc's words. She gave the slightest nod but said nothing.

Wroten stepped back to the center of the room and motioned for Doc to sit.

'What kind of poison . . . ?'

'How . . . ?'

'When . . . ?'

Questions rose from all around. Wroten held up his hand for silence.

'We'll get to that. In a moment. Right now, what is important is that we have two possible suspects sitting right here, and a third man who, while apparently not directly involved, had at least been acting suspiciously.'

All three men — Carver, Lance Prescott, and Roy Mintern — began talking at once.

'You'll each get your chance to talk. For now, shut up and listen to me.'

He turned to Mintern.

'Roy, I've been checking around, and it seems that you've been seen a couple of times in the past couple of weeks, late at night, driving around in your van with Alix Macrorie in the passenger seat. Care to explain.'

Roy looked briefly startled, then a flood of relief crossed his face.

'Is that what this is about? Why you brought me along? I though that since I was there when the body was discovered . . . Well, there's really nothing much to tell.'

'Then it shouldn't take you long,' Wroten said.

'Uh, yes. Well, the fact of the matter is that I've been working late recently, catching up hours so I could take off work days to be with the troop. Elda's pretty understanding about that, but she doesn't want my hours to upset the kids' schedules at home too much, so she figures that on the nights I'm late, I can just pick up my own dinner on the way home. Good Eats is open late most nights, so I just got into the habit of swinging by there every now and again for a bite.

'I knew Alix mostly through her brother Dale. She was a good kid and I recognized her when she waited on me at the restaurant. So a couple of times, when her shift ended and I was there, I gave her a ride home. That's all.'

Wroten stared at him as though expecting him to say more. Mintern swallowed and turned a bit red.

'I mean, that's *all*. A lift home a few

times. We hardly even spoke, and when we did it was usually about how Dale was doing in school or something like that.'

Wroten waited for a beat — he was almost as good at theatrics as Doc was — then: 'So you didn't know about the baby?'

'The . . . what?' Mintern seemed honestly surprised. *Flabbergasted* might be a better word for the expression on his face.

Carver was on his feet.

'Baby? Alix was pregnant?' His face was white . . . and it seemed as if it was drained of color because of anguish, rather than guilt. 'She never told me . . .'

'And that leads us to young Mr. Ellis here.' Wroten turned slightly. He made a small movement with one hand and Deputy Allen grabbed Carver's shoulder and held tight until Carver had resumed his seat.

'I didn't know. She never told me. We only . . . we only did it a couple of times, you know.'

Victoria was watching events closely. She seemed the least surprised of any of us as she gazed gravely at the young man she obviously considered a surrogate son.

I remembered what her friend had reported about Carver and Alix — that he had been 'panting' around the restaurant recently. And doing more than just that, apparently.

Wroten waited patiently.

Finally Carver continued. 'I . . . we were . . . I wanted to marry her, but she said no. I would have married her, too, if I had known that she . . . about the baby. I would have.'

Victoria crossed the room and stood near him, not threateningly but as if to assure him that he had at least one friend in the room. He stared up at her and seemed to speak directly to her, as if she, not Wroten, were the one he needed to convince.

'We've been . . . good friends for years. I loved her. I thought she loved me, too, or I would never have . . . But lately, she had been more . . . distant, I guess. I would talk about making a life for us here, and she would just ignore me. She wanted more, she said. She wanted to get away, go somewhere where she could be someone.

'Then she began dropping hints. There might be someone else, a man who would give her . . . what she wanted.

'I tried to convince her that no one could ever love her as much as I did but . . . '

'But she wouldn't listen, so you got her to come with you up to Porcupine Falls, where you killed her and threw her over onto the rocks.' Wroten's voice came as harshly and as roughly as the granite that had shattered Alix's body.

'No!' Carver tried to surge to his feet again, but this time it was Victoria's gentle hand, not the deputy's sterner one, that restrained him.

'I know, dear. You could never have done that to Alix. You could never have hurt someone you loved.'

'Come on, now, Miz Sears. It all fits. Crime of passion. If he couldn't have her, no one would. Trite, but it happens.' Wroten was speaking directly to Victoria now, Carver for the moment forgotten.

'So he *poisoned* her? That hardly seems like a weapon of choice for such a passionate, irrational killer.'

'Okay, so it is unusual. Poison usually suggests a woman, at least statistically. But maybe he couldn't bear to . . . '

'So he gave her something that made her die in agony, then casually and callously threw her over the falls. Now *that* certainly makes more sense.' For a little old lady, Victoria certainly knew how to wield sarcasm like a knife.

'But it fits the evidence . . . '

'Yes, I know, Deputy Wroten. You've explained all of that to me. And I agree that Alix died of poison, was undoubtedly dead before she was thrown' — for some reason Lance winced at the word, but Carver sat like stone — 'thrown from the cliff.'

'By her murderer,' Doc said. I noted the undercurrents of anger in his voice. He had known Alix, probably had brought her into the world, to use a phrase that Victoria might have used. He wanted her killer found, tried, and punished.

'No,' Victoria said softly.

'What?' That was Wroten.

'No, not by her murderer. You see, Alix Macrorie was *not* murdered.'

9

'Not . . . ' Wroten almost gurgled the word in his surprise and frustration.

'No. At least not in the usual sense of the word. If we must put a legalistic definition to what happened to her, the closest thing I could think of would be . . . well, suicide.'

That startled Carver into action. He started to rise yet again from his chair, his face flushed and the tendons at his neck standing out as if her were about to attack someone. Allen was at his side in an instant. I could see Allen's knuckles fading to white as he pressed against Carver's shoulders; if he didn't know Carver that well, he was probably discovering just how much power and strength lay hidden beneath Carver's plaid shirt and jeans.

For an instant the room froze; I couldn't even hear any breathing, not even my own. Then Carver seemed to collapse. He dropped back into the chair so suddenly that Allen nearly lost his balance. Carver's face drained of blood, and he fixed his eyes on Victoria. She returned his gaze. I could see compassion and love and fear welling in her eyes, and I wondered what she knew that we did not. And how she had discovered it.

The silence lasted for a few seconds more, but when Victoria broke it, she did not speak to Carver, even though she still held his gaze for a moment or two.

'You knew Alix, didn't you, Lance.'

Lance's head jerked around. He had been watching the interplay between Carver and the deputy. Victoria's voice — and her words — apparently caught him completely off guard.

'I . . . well, I . . . no.'

'That's not true, Lance.' Victoria sounded like a doting but sorrowful grandmother who had caught her favourite grandson with his hand in the cookie jar. 'You knew her.'

After a lengthy and uncomfortable pause: 'Yes.'

'And your name isn't really Lance Prescott, is it?'

That struck even further home. She stared at him. Now it was his turn to stare, his skin turning parchment white before flushing crimson. For an instant, I was sure that he would deny it, but his shoulders dropped and he fell back into the chair.

'No,' he said finally, 'it isn't.'

Everyone else in the room looked stunned. Where was this going? What had happened to Wroten's rather straight-line case against Carver?

'It's Bruce Diehl, isn't it.'

This time, amazingly, he grinned. I wouldn't have believed that such a rapid change of emotion could have flickered across a human face, but Lance — or was it Bruce? If Victoria said it was, then it was — Lance almost laughed out loud.

'I guess I should have figured out by now that it's hard to hide anything from you. How did you find out?'

'Oh, I've known for some time now,' Victoria said, repaying smile with smile. 'I may be an old woman, and I may be . . . eccentric . . . but I'm not exactly stupid. When a sturdy young fellow pulls up in my front yard with a jeep loaded with gear, including a couple of high-powered rifles, and asks to spend a few months on my land, I don't always take him at his word. That first day, when you opened your wallet to pay me the rent on the cabin, I caught a glimpse of a name on your license, and it wasn't Prescott. Not enough letters. I didn't see all of the name, but I saw that the last name was Diehl, and, just to be sure — an old woman living alone, you know — I asked a friend of mine to do some checking. The name, plus registration for the jeep — I did get the license number down right — let me know I didn't have anything to worry about.

'It was foolish of you, perhaps, but certainly not criminal. There's no reason that a young man can't want to get away from an overbearing father and a stultifyingly proper family . . . '

'My father isn't . . . ' Lance — Bruce — began, but Victoria cut him off with a wave of her hand.

'Yes he is. I don't know him, but I know the type. New money, old mores.

160

Not a hint of anything but respectability in his son. Best schools. Programmed future. Business all the way. Right?'

Lance (sorry, I just can't think of him any other way) nodded morosely.

'So, an overbearing father and a stultifyingly proper family. As I said, wanting to get away from that is not, by itself, a criminal act. Nor is choosing a rather more . . . well, shall we drop for a moment into colloquialism and say a rather more macho name for one's temporary foray into the great outdoors.'

'Look, Miz Sears,' Wroten said. 'I'm sure this is very interesting and all that, but I've got a murderer to find and . . . '

'I understand, Deputy Wroten. But as I said before, there was no murder . . . at least there was no *murderer*. Lance — you don't mind if I keep calling you that, it is so difficult to think of people with new names once one has an old name firmly engrained in one's head?'

Lance/Bruce nodded mutely.

'Very well. Lance is as close to being Alix's murderer as you . . . '

'I didn't kill her!' Lance was on his feet,

before even Wroten could move. 'I didn't kill her! She was already dead!' He stopped, his body shaking, and even I could see that he was on the edge of collapse. Wroten started toward him but Victoria motioned for the deputy to wait.

'No, my dear,' she said, her voice deep with pity and concern. 'You didn't. Not directly. Perhaps not even indirectly. Certainly not in any way that you could have been aware of. But it is at least in part because of you that Alix MacCrorie is dead.'

'But . . . ' His face was white again, and now the tremors in his arms and hands were obvious. Victoria nodded to Wroten, who crossed the room and helped Lance back into his chair.

'I think I can explain. But you will have to help. You will have to tell the exact truth. I know that you're not proud of what you did, and perhaps there are some legal ramifications that I am not aware of, but you did not murder Alix MacCrorie.'

Lance stared at her.

'You will tell the truth?'

He nodded.

'Very well. To begin with, Lance, you make an abominable mountain man. It was obvious to me from the first moment you stepped foot out of your car that you were not what you wanted to seem. The car was too new, your clothes were too new. Not a scratch on any of the gear I could see through the back window of the jeep. And that ridiculous name. Really! Even if I hadn't peeked at your license, there's no way I would have believed someone looking and sounding like you could really be Lance Prescott. I mean, it was really too much.'

Lance started to protest again, but Victoria held up her hand and continued.

'Oh, please don't be angry. I understand your motives. And quite honestly you did surprise me. I didn't think you would last a week — actually, I rather expected to hear the jeep roaring back down the road and toward civilization sometime during the first night. You simply didn't know enough.

'But you lasted. And you learned. That was what surprised me. You really wanted to learn. A lot of city people come up here, expecting to astonish us natives with your mastery of nature, but you were willing to listen and learn.

'Once in a while, you got a little overbearing — I'm sure *I* got tired of having to eat weeds every time you were anywhere near — but most of the time I was pretty pleased with your progress.'

'Mrs. Sears,' Wroten said, impatient again and wanting either for her to get to the point or for him to be able to leave and get back to the job of finding out what happened to Alix.

'Yes, Deputy. But you have to understand this one point — and understand it clearly — in order to know why Alix died.

'It was obvious to me, and to others as well, those of us who had lived our lives up here, that Lance Prescott was a fake. But a rich fake.

'Now, Lance, tell me about Alix.'

'We . . . we met in the village.'

'In Fox Creek?'

'Yeah. I went in for some supplies and dropped by Good Eats for a . . . well, living off the land was getting a bit tiresome. She was working at the café.

She was . . . nice. Pretty. Young.' He paused for a long moment. 'Nice. I liked her, and I guess she liked me.'

There was a muffled sound from across the room. I glanced over at Carver, who was glaring at Lance, his hands balled into fists. Wroten must have noticed the same thing, because he moved quietly away from Lance, who seemed too wrapped up in his own misery to notice, and stood a yard or so from Carver. Carver didn't notice, either.

'Anyway,' Lance continued, 'there was no one else there, and I invited her to sit with me, and we had coffee and doughnuts and talked. She . . . she was easy to talk to. And I was lonely. I mean, I liked being up at the cabin, being by myself, being in charge of my own life, but it was still pretty lonely, and I . . . I like girls.'

'I'm sure you do,' Victoria said, as sweetly and as primly as if she had been complimenting her nearest neighbor on an unusually fine bottle of preserves. 'And Alix was an unusually likeable young lady.'

'Yeah. Uh, yes. Anyway, one thing led to another, and I agreed to meet her later that night. For a date.'

Carver's response was less muffled this time, but he seemed to have noticed Wroten standing nearby and he didn't make any move to stand.

Instead, he glanced once at Victoria — a look so full of pain and loss that it was heart-wrenching to experience it second hand; I don't think I could have understood what was happening if it hadn't been for Terry and Shawn. I had known loss and heartbreak and the enormity of emptiness, and I now saw it in Carver Ellis's eyes. A glimmer began somewhere in the back of my mind. Carver loved Alix deeply. He had to have. Nothing else could explain his reactions to Lance's explanations. But Carver didn't kill Alix. And, according to Victoria, neither had Lance.

So who did?

'What did you do on your date?' Victoria asked softly, breaking the stillness that had fallen on the room.

'What?' Lance looked up as if startled,

as if he had been lost in memories and did not want to leave them.

'Your date with Alix. What did you do?'

'We . . . we drove around some. She showed me some back roads, took me to a place where you could overlook Fox Creek and see the lights.' He grinned suddenly. The grin made him look ten years younger. 'I'm not stupid, either, Victoria. I knew where we were. We had a Lovers' Lane down home, too. It wasn't as dark or as lonely, it wasn't smack in the middle of a stand of pines that have been standing for a hundred years. But we had one. And I recognized it as soon as we drove up to the edge of the graveled roadway and Alix leaned over and turned off the ignition.'

'What did you do?'

'We . . . we kissed and . . . 'made out' is the term you would use, I guess.'

'Did you . . . ?'

'No,' Lance said quickly, before Victoria could frame her next question. Knowing a little of where Victoria was going, I glanced at Carver. He seemed to relax a bit, just a bit, then tense up again as if he were thinking of something, somewhere other than Lovers' Lane.

'I know it sounds weak, but you've got to believe me. Alix was a nice girl. I liked her. Maybe sometime, if we'd kept seeing each other, we would have . . . But we didn't. Not then. Not ever.'

Victoria studied him for a long while. 'You're more mature than I might have guessed, Lance,' she said finally. 'But Alix wasn't,' she said, her voice softening. I could hear pain in it. 'Alix was pretty and sweet and innocent and loving. But she wasn't mature. She didn't know how to look very far ahead. Probably the only thing she could have told you for certain about her future — the one she had planned for herself — was that it didn't include her remaining in Fox Creek for the rest of her life.

'Isn't that true, Carver?'

He looked up. His eyes were wet with unwept tears. He nodded.

'How do you know?'

'I asked her.'

'Asked her if she was planning on leaving Fox Creek?' That voice was

Wrotens, sounding harsh and awkward after Victoria's gentle softness.

'No, sir,' Carver said, looking up at the man as if thankful for the digression. Then the looked back at Victoria. 'Like I said, I asked her to marry me.'

Victoria nodded and pursed her lips but said nothing. I could see that Carver's confession of love had helped something, some idea to settle.

'And you were hurt when she said no.'

'Yeah, she said no.' Carver looked down again. 'But it wasn't that she didn't love me, she said. It was that she was getting out of Fox Creek.'

'When did you ask her?' Wroten again.

'End of June.'

'When did you first meet Alix, Mr. Diehl,' Wroten asked. Apparently he had had little trouble shifting into using Lance's real name.

'Maybe . . . maybe a week or so before that. Middle of June. But I didn't know she was . . . seeing . . . I didn't know.' He seemed to be appealing to Carver for understanding.

'No, and Alix would have made sure

that you didn't,' Victoria said. 'She could be clever enough when it counted. She had ridden in your car, she had heard your voice and seen your actions, enough to figure out — as I did — that you were not going to stay forever in Fox Creek, that you had somewhere else to go, and wherever that place might be, it was 'civilized.' And she probably had more than an inkling that there was money involved somewhere in your background.'

'Yeah,' Lance muttered. 'I might have . . . she asked about my family, and I wanted to . . . '

'Impress a pretty girl on the first date?' Victoria suggested.

He nodded.

'Well, maybe you're not that mature, after all.'

'But what does this have to do with Alix MacCrorie's death?' Wroten demanded.

'Everything,' Victoria said. 'Simply everything. She wanted out of Fox Creek. Carver had proposed marriage, but she had known him all of her life, knew him well enough to realize that he would never leave the mountains by his own choice.

And she loved him enough not to want to force him to choose between them and her

'Then, just after Carver's proposal had brought things to a head, in walks Mr. Lance Prescott, handsome, virile, strong, an 'older man' who was single and lonely. And — to be fair to Alix — I believe that she was attracted to him as well.

'And then, there was the baby.' She paused for a long while

'Lance, what happened on the day Alix died?'

For a moment he stared at her, then he sighed and nodded. 'It's about time I told. I should have earlier, but I was afraid that if anyone found out ... my father, my family ... '

'They would never have understood, and you were afraid of their reaction?'

'Yes. I was stupid and scared, probably just this side of panic and hysteria, so I did it.'

'Did what, son?' Wroten asked, not as harshly as one might expect.

'I rolled her off the cliff.'

Carver was on his feet and screaming

'Murderer! Murderer!' and Wroten was caught between holding on to Carver, who seemed intent on homicide in front of witnesses, and getting to Lance before he could say anything more. But Allen was quicker than many men would have been in a similar situation, and by the time Wroten had Carver back in the chair, Allen was finishing up.

Reading Lance his rights.

Lance nodded numbly and seemed to collapse even further into his chair.

'Tell us about it,' Victoria urged

'It was Alix's idea, really. I mean, she came up to the cabin that day, all dressed out in hiking gear and an overnighter pack. She wanted to take me into the back country, she said. Past Victoria's property and into the really rugged wilderness inside the National Park. It sounded like a challenge.

'Victoria was right about how much I knew when I came up here. Most of it was bluster. But I had learned a couple of things. I learned that I love it up here. And that I might like to live here for the rest of my life. But most importantly, I had learned that I don't know everything.

'So when Alix agreed to come with me, I figured that, since she was a native up here, she would be able to help if I messed up.'

'That was a mistake,' Victoria said, 'and one that cost Alix her life.'

'But how . . . '

'Never mind for now. What happened?'

'We didn't get far. We went overland, without passing your house, Victoria, to just beyond the meadowlands beneath the falls. I wanted to keep on. The mountains were up ahead; I really felt rugged, capable, and I wanted to get up there and see what there was to see. But Alix seemed tired and wanted to stop.'

Again Victoria nodded.

'Yeah,' Lance said somberly. 'I should have picked up on that. If she was as good as she had claimed, that little hike shouldn't have tired her.'

'That's true. But there was more to Alix's problem than just that. There was the baby.'

'We sat there for a while. It was warm and quiet and peaceful. Beautiful, really.

We talked about . . . I don't remember, we just talked about whatever came up. It was nice.

'Maybe an hour later, we went swimming, then got out and dressed, and Alix said she was hungry. We had agreed to live off the land as much as we could — some more of my pretentiousness, I guess, Victoria — and she started collecting things for lunch. She disappeared for a couple of minutes, along the swampy area by the river, while I got out the lunch things.

'She came back, pleased as punch, with a bunch of Queen Anne's lace, you know, wild carrots.'

Victoria nodded solemnly. 'You loaned her your knife, to dig up whatever she found.' Again, not a question.

'Yes. And I forgot about it until the next night, after she, after the . . . body . . . had been found. I realized that it might be traced to me, so I went back to try to find it.'

'This knife?' Wroten removed the Queen knife from his pocket. 'Yours?'

Lance glanced at it and nodded. 'My

174

dad gave it to me a year ago. I didn't want to lose it, and I didn't want to just leave it lying around.'

'What happened then?' Victoria brought us all back to the tragedy that was unfolding as we listened.

'She'd washed the roots off in the river and was twisting the tops off when she got back. She offered me some, but . . . '

'But what, Bruce?'

I glanced at Victoria, surprised as much by her use of his real name as by her tone of voice. Just hearing it made me want to cry.

'But, well, I'd tried wild carrots a while before, and I broke out in a rash. Hives or something. Allergy maybe. Anyway, I didn't dare eat any more, but she'd gone to so much trouble I felt like a fool. I didn't want to tell her I *couldn't* eat them, so I just said I didn't like them. She giggled and tried to feed one to me, you know, like a mother and a stubborn child. She took a couple of bites and pretended that it tasted yummy.

'Then she got a funny look on her face, and I started to laugh, and pretty soon we

175

were both laughing and everything was okay again. We snacked on trail mix I had brought and headed on up the trail.'

'Toward the falls?' Victoria asked.

'Yes.' By now Lance seemed to expect Victoria to know things that no one else did, because he didn't even pause before continuing the story. 'We climbed up the trail to the falls and crossed the creek on a fallen log a ways further up. It was all scummy with slime and algae. I almost pitched into the river but Alix caught my hand at the last moment and pulled me on across. I was so scared that I almost wet my pants, but Alix thought it was the funniest thing, to see me there with my arms pinwheeling and my feet doing some kind of crazy dance on that log. I guess she didn't really understand how close I was to falling.'

'More than one person has died there,' Victoria said. 'The current right above the falls can be too fast for even a good swimmer, and the rocks up there and at the bottom can be deadly.'

Lance nodded before he continued: 'Anyway, I sat down on a rock to catch my breath, trying to stop the black spots that were spinning around behind my eyes, when Alix started twitching.'

Doc Anderson sat straight up in his chair when he heard that. He shot a glance at Victoria. He and I were probably the only ones in the room that saw her fractional nod. Doc Anderson swallowed hard, but at an almost invisible gesture from Victoria forced himself to sit back.

'What do you mean, Lance?' Victoria asked.

'It was . . . I don't know, I'd never seen anything like it. She started . . . '

'Convulsing?'

'Yeah. I thought for a minute that she might be epileptic or something. I remembered a little from First Aid about epilepsy, you know, loosening the clothing, keeping the tongue from getting bitten off, that sort of things. I guess I hoped that it would pass.'

'But it didn't. It got worse.'

'Was she salivating?' That from Doc Anderson.

'Salivating? Yeah, I guess so. I didn't really notice. The convulsions just kept getting worse. She was in such pain, and I knew that there was no way I could get any help. I mean, our cell phones wouldn't work that far up in the mountains, so we were probably hours from the closest phone or anything — that would be at your place, Victoria.'

She nodded.

'And Alix was getting worse. She was having a harder and harder time breathing. She . . . she wet herself. She was doubled over with the pain most of the time. I sat with her for a long time, I don't know how long, and it got worse and worse, and finally I decided that I would have to go for help because the convulsions weren't stopping. I figured that if it was epilepsy she should have been all right by then

'So I tried to make her comfortable, and got up to head down the trail and . . . '

'And she died,' Victoria said.

'She died.' Lance stared at his hands. 'She died, and I knew she was dead, and there was nothing I could do about it. I . . . I should have gone then for the police or a doctor or something, but I . . . I panicked. If my father got involved, if there was any scandal, I would . . .

'Anyway,' he said after a pause, drawing a deep breath, 'she was dead and I wasn't, so I carried her to the edge of the falls. There the rocks, and the water — I'd noticed them, Victoria, and I figured out how dangerous they could be. So I . . . '

'So you rolled the body off the rocks, hoping that when it was found, everyone would assume that she had fallen and drowned. And you would have been out of it,' Victoria said.

Lance nodded.

10

'Son,' Wroten said quietly, after a moment, 'maybe you'd better not say anything else until you've had a chance to get a lawyer up here.'

Lance looked up, his face furrowed with tears. 'I didn't kill her, sheriff,' he said. 'I didn't.'

'Lance,' Victoria said, drawing his attention back to her. 'The plants that Alix gathered. Did they look like these?' She pointed to the Queen Anne's Lace in the vase across the room.

'Yes,' he said.

'No, I want you to be certain. Look closely and try to remember anything at all that might be different.'

He got up from the chair, stiffly, like an old man, and shuffled over to the vase. Doc Anderson was on the edge of his seat and obviously waiting for something, but I couldn't figure out what. Wroten just looked perplexed, but not enough to move too far away from Carver, who now looked as caved-in on himself as Lance had a few moments before. I followed Lance's movements, and while he studied the flowers, I did likewise.

Queen Anne's Lace. No question. I had seen it often enough growing in Victoria's flowerbeds, I had even seen it growing wild along stream beds, the graceful umbrellas of white flowers nodding over the finely cut leaves. Lance turned to face Victoria.

'That's it. It's the same plant.'

'Lynn, come over here and look closely at this,' Victoria said. I did. I'm not a botanist or anything, but even up close I could tell that it was Queen Anne's Lace. Or at least I was pretty sure it was. I told that to Victoria.

'Describe it, please. Carefully.'

'White flowers, in a kind of umbrella-shape.'

'Umbrel,' she said, nodding.

'Thick stems, with small purple spots.'

'With small purple spots,' Victoria repeated, and Doc Anderson swore softly and stood up.

'What is it?' Lance asked.

'Alix made two mistakes,' Victoria said, as if unaware of Lance's question. 'The first was that she did not know how little Lance actually knew about outdoor survival; she only knew that he seemed obsessed by edible plants, always wandering around eating whatever was close at hand. And the second mistake was, that in her eagerness to please him and impress him, she forgot that she herself did not know much more.

'Doctor Anderson, please tell Lance about this plant.' She closed her eyes and put her hand over them, as if to shut out the light . . . and whatever Anderson was about to say.

'Western water hemlock,' Anderson said, fingering one of the leaves gently.

'But I thought it was Queen Anne's Lace,' I said, not knowing why I should interrupt him but feeling it important that I did.

'I know you did. And so did Lan — Mr. Diehl. And so, apparently, did Alix. But it's not. They look alike, they grow in pretty much the same places, they are members of the same family. They even smell alike. But Queen Anne's Lace is, as

Mr. Diehl noted, really wild carrot and, while not particularly palatable, it is quite edible. Western water hemlock, although a member of the same family as Queen Anne's Lace, is poisonous.'

'The stuff that poisoned Socrates?' Deputy Allen asked, surprising me, perhaps unfairly on my part, with his knowledge of history.

'Similar and related, but not quite the same. In fact, except for the Aamanita mushroom, it is the most poisonous plant in the northern temperate zones.'

Lance's face had gone white again, and Carver was stone-still again, as if not able to believe what he was hearing. Even Wroten seemed stunned. I was probably not in much better shape. Only Victoria was in full command of herself, and she suddenly looked terribly exhausted — emotionally as well as physically.

Anderson continued, his voice taking on a dispassionate, distanced lecture tone that, I am sure, was at least unconsciously intended to defuse some of the horror of what we were hearing. 'All parts of the plant are dangerous, including the leaves and stems. Children have died after making whistles or peashooters from the stems. But the roots are the most deadly part. In some parts of the country, the plant is called cowbane. I've heard that a piece of root the size of a walnut can kill a full-grown cow inside half an hour.

'It's as poisonous to humans. One case I heard of, a man found what he thought were wild artichokes growing in some land he was clearing. He ate a couple. And died two hours later. It's that poisonous.

'There's spasms, tremors; convulsions, extreme stomach pain, dilated pupils, frothing at the mouth, delirium. And death. Usually from exhaustion and the inability to breath.' He stopped. No one else felt like speaking.

'Shit,' Allen whispered, then glanced around to see if anyone would take offense at his language. No one did. We all felt the same.

'So,' Victoria said finally, 'Alix was not murdered. She killed herself without knowing it. And Lance — Bruce — could not have stopped her. He was wrong in what he did later, but as Doctor

Anderson is no doubt willing to testify, Alix was dead before her body went over the falls. There is little doubt of that. Bruce may still be in for some difficulties over his actions after her death, but, Deputy Wroten, I am certain that he did not know why she died.'

Everyone waited for Wroten to say something.

'I came out here to find a murderer,' he said at last. 'I thought I had three possibilities. I could have made some kind of case for each of them, I suppose.

'I didn't expect a fourth to appear out of nowhere. Or that it would be the victim herself.'

He motioned toward Carver and Mintern.

'As far as I'm concerned, you two are free to go.'

Neither moved, but it seemed that a look of relief crossed Roy Mintern's face. Carver still sat rock-like, stunned. Alix dead. His unborn child dead. It was a great deal for a young man like him to accept. I wasn't sure he ever would.

'As for Mr. Lance-Bruce Prescott-Diehl, I'm going to hold you for a while. There may be a charge of tampering with a body, obstructing an investigation into a mur . . . a suspicious death . . . '

'But certainly under mitigating circumstances, don't you think?' Victoria added.

Wroten didn't answer her.

Everyone else left a few minutes later, crowded in the deputy's car. Carver and Mintern would have to make official statements, and Doc would need to complete an official autopsy report, but essentially the case was closed.

Victoria and I remained in her living room.

She picked up her knitting and began again, *clack, clack, clack.*

Finally I broke the silence.

'I think I had better get on back to Estelle's cabin. It's been quite a visit, though, even if a bit longer . . . and rather more eventful . . . than I anticipated yesterday morning.'

'Yes, so it has.'

'And to think that yesterday when I woke, I was amazed at how deliciously quiet and peaceful it was up here in the mountains.'

She didn't say anything.

'Thank you,' I added.

'Why, for what, Lynn dear?'

'I know you didn't plan for any of this to happen. The scouts finding Alix and all. But I have a feeling that even if it hadn't, you would have made sure that I would not have felt alone yesterday.'

She laid the knitting aside.

'I would have tried. I've been there, suffered loss, known how long it took for life to reassert itself. I had intended simply to keep you company, show you around the place, chat for a while.

'As things turned out, we did a bit more than that.'

We both laughed lightly.

'And besides, Lynn dear, I did so want you to meet Lance . . . oh, drat! I suppose I mean, Bruce. I hoped he might drop by for a visit. He's such a nice young man.'

THE END

Western Water Hemlock is a highly toxic member of the parsnip/carrot family, many of whose other species are edible. It is among the most poisonous species of plant life in the Northern Hemisphere, and has been labeled the 'most violently toxic plant that grows in North America' by the USDA. It is a relative of the hemlock species used to kill Socrates.

It is also known as: Musquash Root, Spotted Cowbane, Beaver Poison, Spotted Water Hemlock, and Common Hemlock.

TOMORROW, UTOPIA

Steve Hayes and David Whitehead

In Washington a high-ranking politician is murdered, whilst in Central Africa, a new virus is killing thousands of male victims. And on the internet, a group known as The Utopians grows in power. Is there a connection between all these things? Homicide Detective Ben Hicks, however, has his own problems. Meanwhile, Pentagon cryptologist Hunter McCormack witnesses the murder of a politician. Now the killers are out to silence *her* . . . and no one believes she saw the killing. Except Ben . . .

THE PLOT AGAINST SHERLOCK HOLMES

Gary Lovisi

When Sherlock Holmes finds himself enmeshed in the most deadly case of his career, it threatens to bring terrible doom upon him and his friend Doctor John H. Watson. A deadly nemesis from his past, a most vile and evil villain, has returned to England to wreak his revenge for past deeds. He unleashes a dastardly plot, which begins with a shocking murder in Whitechapel and causes Inspector Lestrade to believe that Jack the Ripper has returned . . .

CLOSELY KNIT IN SCARLATT

Ardath Mayhar

Olive, 'The Knit Lady,' is an unlikely secret agent. A professional assassin and in her sixties, she had been quietly recruited by 'The Brokers.' Now she is hired to kidnap and kill retired British agent Benjamin Scarlatt, but Olive has scruples. And when an Islamic terrorist group takes over the cruise ship on which both she and Scarlatt are travelling, she fights back with knitting needle, scalpel and plastic explosives — proving that it's dangerous to underestimate Little Old Ladies!